AS FAR AS THE MIND MAY DREAM

MICHAEL BOOKOUT

Dedication:

To the Silence to the Eternal

'As far as the Mind may Dream' © Michael Bookout 2009

CONTENTS

Introduction:

AND IT CAME TO PASS IN THE CALENDAR MONTH of February 1923, a time in the British Isles where it would not be unusual to find husbands, wives and their children, spending endless hours at home enjoying each others' company, while unbeknownst to them, a girl child was born whom, in her own way, would change the course of British history.

Those ignorant inhabitants (innocent as they were) sat in their comfortably furnished parlors, piecing together colorful picture puzzles with infinite shapes that came together making lovely landscape pictures or ones with as fluffy kittens.

They would also line up in straight order on a feather sofa while mother or father read from the adventures of David Copperfield, a fictional character; a young man whom at a very early age had fallen in love with a person whom he related to as: 'Poor Emily' .

And on they read turning the pages from Gothic tales; tales that wend their way deep into the Bavarian woods where misguided, young children were devoured by voracious wolves or witches with gnarly faces pinpointed by warts, and streaming puss, whose personalities fit the temperament of 'perverse disposition' .

But this simple, comfortable description of something that appears as a happy home life was not the profile of Mr . and Mrs. Tumblers the occupants of the Polstar Manor, London , England .

The manor took its name from the renown stone known as Polstar Emerald a gem which had an almost mythical reputation. Some time in the 14th century Wales the stone appeared in the domain of a royal family and, then within the next century it fell into the possession of a merchant of fabulous wealth residing in Persia. The stone would then disappear altogether, years later landing in the palm of a child scourging for clams on a deserted beach and then thru a foggy series of thefts, blackmails and even murder it was discovered in the Ethiopian forests being used as an all-seeing eye in the cranium of a temple idol.

And from the many years of its first unearthing in what had been rumored, the south eastern slopes of the Pyrenees mountains (a time before the 14th century) the Polstar stone was, at the unfolding of our story, to all the world invisible. But invisible did not mean it had altogether vanished. Rather, the stones existence, as was suspected, by those who by craft of sluth had followed its life course, now believed it to be resting in the home of Mr. and Mrs. Tumblers in a steel enclosure.

The Tumblers were a senior couple without children who kept to themselves spending most of their days and evenings facing one another in the high-backed chairs of their sitting room while the fire in the hearth smoldered a dull orange .

Mr. Tumblers was referred by his devoted wife, Edna as 'Old Toad', a man whom she had married when they were of the equal age twenty one and had lived in their home for so many years it was not in either of their best interest to count or divide or in anyway reminisce about

the thousands of hours, seconds, and days that both husband and wife set about the simple task of taking up space for the basic cause of animal survival.

Sadly both Mr. and Mrs. Tumblers wondered obsessively about all the past years and the many dreams for a glorious life and how they had scampered off in opposite, irretrievable directions.

And every day husband and wife observed their mate with keen interest questioning which of them would be the survivor and watch who was lowered into the grave first?

From the day of Toad's retirement as bank president, husband and wife began to learn with precise timing where the other one would be at precisely every moment of the day and what he or she would be doing for the length of that task.

Mr. Tumblers knew that Mrs. Tumblers would rise from bed and give a few groans in response to the mounting assault of rheumatism in her joints, slip on her slippers and robe, go immediately into the kitchen to boil a pot of tea water, and while that was steaming she would wash her face in the bathroom sink, fluff her hair, tighten her bathrobe, yawn, then toddle back to the kitchen, and prepare apricot juice, toast, marmalade, and butter.

All this she did in expectation of having a few moments to herself with the morning newspaper before "Old Toad" as she sometimes referred to Mr. Tumblers, would rise to pester her the remainder of her waking hours.

Mrs. Tumblers on the other hand had categorically observed Toad and watched him each morning stretch, yawn two great yawns, tighten his bathrobe, comb what little of his hair remained with a pearl handled brush inherited by his even toadied father: Toad Senior, and some mornings top off this mundane routine by belching like an old cow.

Toad would then pester about in the kitchen pouring tea, looking over his wife's shoulder to read the news headlines, butter his toast, and then go kindle a fire , sit in his stuffed chair, and switch on the radio to the classical music station interrupted by the top-of-the-hour news.

From the time they arose, there would be an approximate two and one half hours until the morning dishes were cleared, showers taken, and a few mutual complaints about the cold weather were shared that the Tumblers found themselves' sitting in their overstuffed chairs staring blankly.

The one portion of the Tumblers day that intercepted their tedium of quiet desperation was when Toad excused himself with a theatrical 'harrumph' and then rise to make his way out the back double doors to tend to his pristine garden. And in some mechanical way this was the signal for Mrs. Tumblers to put a shawl across her shoulders and leave through the front manor entrance to see what packages or letters may be awaiting her at the post box .

And it so happened the very day this story begins, this January twenty sixth day, that Mrs. Tumblers upon walking the few paces down the cobblestone path discovered a rather misshapen basket containing a small child wrapped in an unusually colorful blanket lying in it.

Mrs. Tumblers first reaction was to look around for the mother of this child but, alas there was no mother to be seen and no father or guardian of any sort. Upon second glance to this seemingly

abandoned baby Mrs. Tumblers pulled back the colorful blanket noticed it possessed enormous, attentive green eyes that shone with the force and fire equal to that of any piece of jewelry displayed in the Tower of London collection.

Had anyone person at this point observed Mrs. Tumblers reactions they would not have believed what they had seen when this woman whom had not let one day of the last fifteen years of her life go by without complaint of rheumatism, bent at the waist with great agility, and in one sweeping motion picked up the baby, basket and all. Mrs. Tumblers, Edna then pressed the child close to her stomach with her shawl protecting it from the cold, and hurried with great rapidity back to the manor where she slammed the front door, and latched it with great passion!

When Toad came through the back double doors in his stocking feet several hours later, having left his mud covered shoes outside, he placed on his slippers and walked over to his wife whom only he, after having seen her in that very chair for so many countless hours noticed she was sitting in a posture that was not her normal pose. Before Mr. Tumblers could ask the most obvious and predictable question of "Are you right, my Dear?", he intuitively held silent when he observed the misshapen basket on the floor and a child neatly wrapped in clean cloth placed evenly on Mrs. Tumblers footstool.

"Sit down my Dear", instructed Mrs. Tumblers to her husband Toad using a tone with her voice which Toad could not quite place but remembered having heard it's eerie sound before.

Mr. Tumblers moved gingerly to his chair and sat without a ruffle noting that the classical radio program was turned off, and that his wife was staring with the greatest intensity at the child.

"I don't know her proper name as there was no note left on the basket. I call her a 'she' as I have just finished giving her a bath. Thankfully she seems quite healthy, possessing the muscular makeup I would expect on a boy, though she is most assuredly a girl," explained Edna.

"Toad, don't you see .. ?" began Edna using that eerie voice which at that moment struck Toad as being the one he had tried very hard in his life to leave behind.

Toad recalled one unforgettable afternoon in his days of his employment that he had found Edna sitting just as edgy as he observed her sitting now.

"There had been an accident," and this was all his young wife needed say. Mr. Tumblers recognized a grave, uneasiness in her voice, and understood that his wife could only be referring to an accident involving their only child, a daughter who was five years old, and in someway, and somehow, she left this world, and would never return.

"She has come back to us my Dear! Only a mother would know", said Edna who was now looking at Toad with a most curious crook on her lips, her eyes wide and watery, and both her hands gripped hard upon the armrests of her chair .

"Look, Toad," she said with her voice now racing, "do you remember the dimples , how the corners of the mouth turned up? The eyes. Look! You can most definitely see it in the eyes! It is She Toad; she has come back to us! "

Poor Mr . Tumblers. Poor Old Toad. It would not be he, who would tell his wife the truth. Heavens! At her age it would crush her heart, perhaps be her fateful undoing altogether.

Certainly over the years he had played tricks in his mind wishing the massive Pulsar Manor to be a place for himself and him alone but in reality he would be lost without his wife whom in the depths of his heart he loved.

"Why, who could make my tea as perfectly as Edna?" he asked himself rather wounded. "And I could never manage washing my shirts or ironing them. Oh, cruel life! No, this would not do at all; not at all." And so Toad purposed to indulge Mrs. Tumblers as well he could, by responding to the situation saying "Well my dear, we should consider feeding her something."

"You tired Old Toad don't you think I have already considered this?" snapped Edna. "There's water boiling in the stewing pot, and a canning jar with milk in it heating. Don't you think I know how to tend to my own child?"

"Now I want you to go into the attic and resurrect the crib," commanded Edna with a wince in her voice.

"Yes , Dear," groveled Toad but remained sitting, staring at the child.

"Well, what are you waiting for Mr. Tumblers?" snapped Edna again.

Toad cleared his voice and said lightly "Might we not have a name for the child, dear?

Mrs . Tumblers let out a deep breath of exasperation. "Did you think I intended to let my child go through her life without a name?"

And of course Mr . Tumblers knew his wife would supply the child with a name, it was just that he wondered if it would be the same name; the name of their daughter who had been gone for fifty years?

"Actually my dear…" he bumbled on.

Mrs. Tumblers shot poor Toad a glance so direct it would be fair to surmise had an elephant sustained the same look the elephant would stop in its tracks and fall over dead .

"Isabella Rose", said Mrs. Tumblers with determination. "There, if it will satisfy you that I have thought of a name for my girl she shall have her original name, Isabella Rose."

This was not the name Mrs. Tumblers had given their first daughter reasoned Toad, and yet, he wondered why his wife had so rapidly settled on such a compelling, and, in a poetic sense, such a beautiful name?

There are explanations for events like these when persons like the Tumblers, who are thrown into unplanned, uncharted circumstances such as receiving a breathing child on the cobblestone path of their home, and having to somehow place this new arrival into their daily routines.

With such emergencies the human mind no matter how senior can rise to a challenge of unexplainable proportions and in the situation of Mrs. Tumblers in need of a name, she unwittingly named the infant a secret name, one that had not been spoken of in the isles of Britain for many centuries: Isabella Rose.

"May I ask my dear, what is the origin of this selection? It has the ring of something not of common day usage? "It" and here Toad used one of his annoying jesters by putting his fist softly to his lips while clearing his voice indicating he was approaching a potentially offensive phrase, "it seems a bit difficult, if I may be reflective?"

"Tell me something easy about this life, Toad and I shall change my child's name to Lily Flower, or Easter Bunny," railed Edna. She shall have the name Isabella Rose, Mr. Tumblers, and there will be nothing more said of the matter! And now I believe I have instructed you to bring down the crib, have I not?"

Poor Toad was so upset and unsettled about this 'child business' as he in time would refer to it, he forgot to utter his customary "harrumph" while lifting from his chair which he had taken refuge in and walked back out to his garden. And almost as if it was not his place to do so Toad took a fleeting glance at Isabella's enormous green eyes.

"Isabella shall have the best of everything", contemplated Edna as she sat in the bedroom and in the rocking chair she once nursed with her first daughter. Isabella was safe in Edna's arms and with her head nestled deep into Edna's breast breathed at a constant pace.

Edna let fly across her mind the voice of that child of five; the sometimes crying but more often the carefree laughter of someone joyful in spirit who felt safe from the dreadfulness of the world.

There was a small garden before Edna and she looked out the room's large, north facing window catching her own self in reflection as she bobbed back and forth in her chair. "In several hours Toad will have brought down the crib, scrubbed with cleaning solvent and when it is dry I will place fine linen for the child to lie upon."

It was not unusual for Edna to speak out to herself when she was alone, and often times over the course of their lives, Toad had walked in upon her as she sat stitching on the sofa or completing tasks around the Manor thinking his wife had invited a visitor to tea and the two of them were about to come to blows over one subject or another.

"There is no doubt all will be well for my Isabella Rose", said Edna again to the walls, window and ceiling of the room.

"I shall be most vigilant to care of her; fight for her safety; die for her if the necessity presents itself. The world will not have it's opportunity's to take my child from me this time; I shall employ all of my skills, all of my life's lessons to this end. And Toad shall be at my disposal every step of the path. Every step I say; even if I have to crack a whip across his back!"

Chapter I

The Girl with the Emerald Green Eyes

The morning sunlight floated through the dew covered windowpane and intermixed with lace curtains of Isabella's bedroom like tiny feathers coughed from clouds releasing their load so they might float higher.

Isabella woke from her sleep, and hoping out of bed with the greatest dexterity moved as she had for the last year directly to the window ledge where she nestled down on the pillows that lined the divan and pulled her nightgown tight around herself.

Isabella's habit was to part the lace curtains and put forth her right hand while extending her index finger placing it at the center of her face on the crest of her forehead. And with her other index finger she placed it on the middle windowpane and began to simultaneously trace the outline of her face with her finger on the moistened, dew speckled glass.

Isabella had come to greatly admire the visage mirrored back to her, drawn with parted dew drops on the morning which just happened to be that of a young lady who was to celebrate her eleventh birthday.

She so admired the strong, fine, structure of her facial bones, and how they commingled to present a strikingly handsome face; her bones draping with an olive oil skin which kept its natural bronze veneer even though the British fog rarely let the sun shine .

She thought this exercise in narcissism something all persons of royalty must do as a reminder that the care and good will of themselves reflected directly upon the subjects and lands of their rule.

"And being a Princess was not such a bad thing to wake up to on your birthday," said Isabella to herself, and not without indifference, for having her bedroom in the 'Turret Lookout' of the Polstar Manor was a gift she had given herself when she had turned ten.

This turret room was a gabled extension rising above the common roof some twenty feet high which faced London's West side and looked out towards Hyde Park Gate and onto Kensington Gardens beyond.

There was also to the West, the view down onto Toad's garden, the glass enclosed trellis and cultivated dirt rows where multiple displays of rose flowers and vegetables had been planted and were in various stages of growth. And surrounding the trellis, and the yard altogether, was a high thicket of sweetbriar which would soon integrate itself as a significant object for Princess Isabella's destiny.

And of course there was Isabella's favorite feature of the turret outlook; the hidden staircase leading down from her bedroom which could not be seen from the exterior of the building and had a hidden door entrance that opened up into Toad's library.

"Princess Isabella" was the title her parents addressed her by for as many days as her mind might dream and she used this title to commandeer the possessions she desired such as taking eminent domain of the turret.

Isabella learned all she needed to know about being of royal lineage while sitting on the sofa with one or both of her parents as they read to her from the Tumbler's bulging library.

She had spent many an hour there listening with great delight as Toad and Edna cast their voices with inventive dexterity into the rolls of historical or fictional Kings and Queens of national fame .

There were the thrilling accounts of wars and ferocious, fabulous battles which took place between England and its foes. And within these mixtures of armament and persons came passions of lost hope, betrayal among the closest of friends; mothers who wept for their deceased children, wives kissing their husbands for what either of them knew might be the final time before battles began.

The pageantry of it all; grand parades with frolicking horses, minstrels, a cacophony of musicians with cannons saluting in recognition for their potentates! And of course there were the festive balls where hundreds of guests showed off their finery, laughing and dancing, while secret lovers stole kisses in shadowy porticos, as their chambermaids kept protective watch.

There were also the pampered princes and princesses; absolutely to Isabella's liking. While princes learned the ways of war, princesses were instructed in clothing and to be charming ornaments at the disposal of their men. Unless of course, the princess was of an exceptional beauty and need do more than to accept accolades and dismiss marital proposals!

Isabella knew that these princesses were valued to the extent that entire armies set against one another had her name been offended or her life threatened.

"But Isabella!" pleaded both her mother and her father for her safety while using the secret stair well. "With less than one misstep Isabella Rose you could easily cripple yourself."

Yes, Isabella could easily had tread unevenly upon anyone of the one hundred and thirty stairs walking up to the turret lookout room, and just as easily tread unevenly again while coming down (which of course would be the total number of two hundred and sixty potential twisting of the ankle bones or catching a toe causing her to fly headlong down).

But Isabella was insistent about her right of secret passage and had long mastered the facial looks incumbent upon the holder of her office of rule. With the least movement of her muscles she could signal her precise demands.

When Isabella held rigid her posture, made stoic her face, emphasized by the clamping of her jaw; and then as she lowered her head that her brows covered her eyes as if she had no eyes at all, Isabella gave the notion that she was in no mood for compromise.

And so the fourth floor lookout with its own stairwell, its private view down onto to Toad's garden, and a bird's eye view of all of London's exclusive West End had become the place Isabella chose to lay her head each night .

And now that she was awake she wondered again on this foggy English morning what gift she would give herself for this, her eleventh birthday?

Isabella, once having entered the dining hall found Edna had cooked an exceptionally wonderful breakfast of bangers and eggs and laid out a variety of marmalades with which to cover their toast as all three of the Tumbler's spoke about the delicious aroma coming from the oven where the three layer chocolate cake was baking.

As Isabella was finishing with her meal Edna did the traditional thing, excusing herself to the hall closet and returning with a variety of beautifully wrapped gifts of varying sizes and with ornamental bows intertwined in invented shapes.

These were put before a beaming Isabella who listened as both her parents sang the happy birthday song. The largest of the gifts was as always placed to the left of Isabella and then succeeded in front of her in diminishing size to her left.

There were several dresses, a pink scarf made of silk, several blouses and and a tiara made mostly of a thin clay with shiny costume jewels and thin supporting wire. But Isabella's favorite present would be the one she called her magic charm bracelet.

It fit perfectly around her wrist with its smooth silver design and a variety of dangling images.

There was a rabbit, a seal, a dolphin and a fine boat all of them carved with precise proportion.

"Oh mother!" exclaimed Isabella as she jumped from her chair to embrace her mother. "I love them all!" Isabella then navigated around the table to give Toad a hug and a kiss as well.

And then it was Toad's turn as he harrumphed himself back from the table and stood exclaiming that he was going to his labyrinth and invited Isabella to join him on another traditional adventure. This once per year journey of just father and daughter had begun when Isabella was six.

Off they strode to Toad's library, Toad holding Isabella's hand as if he were guiding her on a nature walk with the pretend possibility they might encounter a tiger or hostile tribesmen. And there at the back of the room just opposite of the staircase Toad initiated a slight push upon one of the bookends which caused a section of the bookcase to swivel silently upon a hinge and open into a darkened hallway.

Toad then reached up pulling on a cord lighting the hallway before them. Isabella still holding Toad's hand played her part in the adventure by saying what she had on that first birthday "Are we going to a book cemetary Toad?" To which Toad replied "No my dear, something more like an ancient crypt".

And it might very well be a crypt, as once down the dim hallway they walked down a thin stairwell of uneven stones and then, with the pulling of another cord a subterranean room opened up to them. This then was Toad's private room of Masonic imagery emphasised by ancient Egyptian artifacts.

Even at age six Isabella had been overwhelmed by the enchanted feeling enveloping her as she stepped from the stairwell onto the masses of Persian carpets which stretched to each corner of the long rectangular room. There were also wonderfully thick carpets draping down the walls. Of the furnishings there were soft silken chairs and couches with which Isabella sank into wondering if she might sink in over her head. And as Isabella wandered round what was something of a miniature museum, Toad ignited overhead incense hangers which emitted strange scents that presented a mysterious mood giving the effect of having been transported back thousands of years.

And then there were the artifacts. The capes, caps and apron signifying Toad's ranking in the Masonic lodge, a cane and different instruments of measure, these all Isabella had learned of and took only slight interest. But when she came to behold the mummified corpse in a glass enclosure of someone person Toad told her must have been a child due to its small stature, Isabella let out a small gasp of incredulity and placed her hands over her mouth as children of age six do and backed away from the enclosure where the figure lay.

And as Toad beheld Isabella with great delight and while laughing he turned his attention to a free standing wood and iron table off in the corner. Toad pushed slightly upon an area of the table as the top slid open revealing the door and lock to a safe.

Toad spun the numbers of the lock and then with precision clicked each mechanism of the tumblers into their respective niche. 'Click' remembered Isabella and then the full revolution of the dial and 'click' again. Two more revolutions in the opposite direction and the final 'click' released the encryption thus opening the door. Toad reached in daintily pulling out a leather box with an ivory clasp which he flipped open and instructed Isabella to sit on the couch next to him.

"And this my dear is for you," said Toad placing a small, heavy and highly polished stone into Isabella's upturned, outstretched palms.

"A gem stone, Toad? Is this more jewelry from ancient Egypt?" inquired Isabella with glee.

"Yes my dear. As you remember me sharing with you that before meeting your mother, I did a bit of traveling to the Far East. I was young and robust and several chaps and I went on an expedition with several guides near Cairo."

"We of course were very naughty going back one night, back to one the places we had visited and this time without our guides. All of us helped ourselves to many gemstones from a little guarded museum. I of course purchased many of the artifacts we have here but of this beauty I am afraid I pinched."

"By the time I arrived home in England I had begun to feel whispers of guilt for the portion of gems I had taken and vowed one day that after my studies were finished at university I would return to Egypt and replace my booty. But how time slipped by and soon I was involved in the world of finance and so here they sit today at the Pulstar Manor."

"But Toad, you could have mailed them back to Egypt," said Isabella naively.

To which Toad burst out with uncommon laughter. "Oh my child. How innocent you are. Those gems stones would have been stolen by anyone of a thousand persons along the path back to that tiny museum. No my

Pet, in some wonderful way I do believe they are in much better care here with our family and in safe keeping for your inheritance.

"What stone is it father?"

"This is an emerald," replied Toad with pride. "Isn't it magnificent my child!" Now let us go upstairs that you may show your mother what gift you have."

And while showing off her stone to Edna, Isabella was reminded that she may never go to Toad's crypt alone and never tell another soul that she had been there. She was also informed that Toad once again, as with all her other gifts, had to put the stone back into the safe as it was very valuable and just like in the story of Aladdin, pirates might come and steal it.

And so Isabella begrudgingly gave Toad back her stone after holding it only briefly. She again did give her vow about not visiting the crypt alone but year upon year, and with each of her birthdays which seemed to stretch out further in the distance, Isabella became more and more passionate about investigating the crypt all by herself.

"Come now my dear," said Toad to Isabella once they had had their fill of the birthday feast . "I do believe the centifolia roses will be at the height of their blossom and the Dutch province are giving off the most fragrant scents.

As Toad helped his daughter with her garden shoes, Edna proclaimed that she hoped Isabella might gather together a bouquet to form the centerpiece at this evenings supper; "I do believe Mr. Tumbler's and I shall be entertaining someone of great importance," she said merrily.

Toad and Isabella walked the few feet down the garden path when Toad stopped at the row of lettuce and bent on one keen to take in hand a few leaves.

"We have had a visitor to our garden since last we were here my dear."

"Who would that be father?" said Isabella arching her head around not really expecting that an elf or a Nome had walked about the planted rows casting spells to help their plants grow but pretending curiosity just the same.

"Bend down here next to me and you can touch them yourself," her father said. "We see it has been a rabbit again? See here; no plant virus could have caused these jagged edges, nor is it the work of worms. Rabbits without a doubt; we shall have to put up a fence; they must have burrowed in under the bramble."

As Toad went into the trellis to gather stakes and cut swaths of canvas to nail to them, Isabella who was still in the bent over position fussing with the leaves and soil, put back her hand to balance herself and in so doing placed her fingers onto the softest surface she had ever touched.

"Are you are a rabbit?" asked Isabella in a friendly tone before actually turning her head to identify what she was touching. The softness Isabella felt was indeed the hair of a rabbit and Isabella made the immediate presumption that she and the rabbit would become wonderful friends.

Isabella sat fully upon the damp grass and shifted her body so that she was facing the bunny. Isabella with the greatest care placed a hand on the rabbit's back to pet it and just as indifferently as when she had first touched it, the rabbit made no effort to move.

Isabella picked a full leaf of lettuce, and with one hand coupling the vermin simultaneously tempted it, while pulling it to her breast.

"Got yourself a new acquaintance there?" said Toad.

"Yes, Father; he is my new friend."

"But I'm afraid we can't allow these rodents to eat our food can we Isabella?" he said coming upon her with a menacingly large mallet. "Please Isabella, let it down; if we let this one live he'll be back with others of his kind."

"No daddy, I love this rabbit!" shouted Isabella holding up her free arm to stop Toad's progression.

"Honey, it's for the best; really, if we let this one go it's only a matter of time before the entire garden is ruined."

"No Toad!" said Isabella determinedly as she drew the rabbit even closer to her breast while simultaneously standing in defiance "you won't kill Admiral Nelson."

"I guess you leave me no choice, my Dear," said Toad resignedly knowing he would never win a contest pitted against a princess. "It appears you and your friend have won the day."

A moment or two lapsed when this testing of wills had subsided before Toad asked his daughter, "How indeed did you arrive at the name of Admiral Nelson so quickly; are you sure the rabbit is a gentleman bunny?"

"Of course he is father, he told me so," said Isabella nestling the little bunny, and petting it with great care .

"It's not like one of your dolls, Honey," advised Toad. "It won't stay put on the shelf when you go off to play with other things; it could run away at any time."

"I think Admiral Nelson wants to live with us father; he has no reason to run away."

"Well," said Toad "your 'friend' Admiral Nelson is certainly welcome to play with you any time he wishes, but we can't have him eating our vegetables. Here, I have the stakes; I'll need you to hold them."

Isabella put her new friend on the ground while it finished eating the portion of lettuce she had given it, and took the stake Toad handed her.

Toad spoke delicately while he instructed Isabella how to position the stake as she half listened and strained the rest of her attentions to the movement of Admiral Nelson.

Once Toad began pounding the stake Isabella turned her attentions more from her father as Admiral Nelson finished with his morning meal and began hopping to the hole he had carved for himself in the sweet briar bramble.

"Where are you going?" asked Isabella turning from Toad's clanking mallot as it hit the fence stake. Isabella let go the stake and shifted herself running and then crawling after her rabbit touching it's hind leg only momentarily before it disappeared completely beneath the thicket .

"I am coming Admiral Nelson; please wait!" cried Isabella .

The sweetbriar had a new bloom of light pink flowers and the thistles which gave the bramble its reputation of formability, and pricked at Isabella's hands as she tried parting the hole large enough to let herself in. Isabella winced at the pricks on her skin but continued to go forward until she finally made her way to an opening that was something like a cavern similar to one found inside a mountain only much, much smaller.

Isabella thought she heard Admiral Nelson move a few paces in front of her and proceeded deeper into the bramble which, as she continuing a few feet more, found that it opened into a much larger cavern. This second cavernous formation was much denser on its outside surface shuttering out the light altogether .

For the moment Isabella forgot about the chase she was giving her Admiral, and began feeling her way around the parameters of the interior of the shrub imagining it to be an ancient cathedral or perhaps more appropriately, a castle gathering hall on the Themes.

The floor of the shrub cavern was flat, and there were no rocks or tree roots to obstruct her movement or to stumble over. And as Isabella stood, her mind immediately whisked away with complex thoughts about the styles of chandelier she would install to illuminate the room and what she would call her throne room (as she had already decided it was to be the receiving hall of a royal court) and She, the Just, and equitable ruler, with animal as well as bird and insect subjects to adore her.

Her "children" as she would address her subjects, would be of the gentry and poor alike, and bring to her gifts, and tidings and solicitations of such varied formulas that she would have to dig deep into her own integrity to conjugate appreciation and give wise answers to their multitude of queries.

Isabella may have been drifting on for more than three days about her new found castle keep when she heard her name called : "Isabella," called out Toad with a strain in his voice "Where are you my dear; Isabella, are you gone missing?"

"I am here father," cried out Isabella from her receiving hall, and then lowering herself back onto her hands and knees made her way into the morning fog-light, out into the garden .

"There you are, " said Toad attempting to cover over his concern about the possible need of having to explain to his wife about losing the child, "off exploring have you been? I don't know that the bramble bushes are the best thing to be lurking about ; the thorns can get rather vicious by the season's end; and heavens! my Dear, look at your clothing ."

 "Oh, father, " exclaimed Isabella with equal enthusiasm of a young girl who had uncovered a long neglected chest with beautiful porcelain dolls , and finely crafted ceramic toy horses. "I have discovered my lost castle, Father ! Would you like to come and see?"

"In time my dear, of course, but for now I still require your assistance putting up this fence." Isabel once again took hold of a wooden stake Toad handed her, and began reflecting in a more

serious way than she had to this point in all her young life, why her parents had not yet confided in her how they knew for certain she was a real princess?

Undoubtedly, she reflected, this title had been given to many a child, in many a language throughout the world, and throughout world history. Though how many of those children lived in an English manor, had as their bedrooms a castle turret, and essentially had both the Duchess Edna, and Duke, Old Toad, to wait upon them?

As Isabella continued to ruminate, her mind jaunted over to the quick witted writings of Mr. Lewis Carol's which are found among the chapters of his famous story: ' Through the Looking Glass -the Adventures of Alice in Wonderland'.

"Was not her rabbit, Admiral Nelson, a clue to a story that would be written about me?" questioned Isabella not in the least concerned that she was putting herself into a lofty position of potential world fame.

"Will I as well, have similar adventures as Alice had when she was a little girl; and won't girls such as me sit with their fathers and mothers listening to stories about my life, and my adventures?"

As Toad pounded in the last of the stakes, and began to staple the limp meshing that would serve as the barrier against invading bunnies, there was as it were, a light gone off in Isabella's mind; an emerald light to be exact, much as if she were looking from inside herself and seeing all her future life that was to come to her.

"Indeed," thought Isabella "there can be no mistake; my life will be like that of Alice; it shall be a real-life fairytale!"

It was at the exact moment that Toad had pounded the last fastener to the last stake, when

Edna called from the back doors informing them that soup was on the table and going from warm to cold.

"Just look at your clothes , Isabella," said Edna as Isabella came up the steps to the door; her beautiful cotton dress with pink satin sash, spotted with mud, and frayed on the edges from having contact with the bramble.

"Good Heavens, Child," exclaimed Edna "you are looking the part of a Gypsy girl! If you insist on digging in the dirt with your father we are going to have to stitch you clothes that match your meanderings. I am shocked Isabella, truly shocked that you haven't taken better care."

Edna sent her daughter to wash and change into cleaner clothes and when Isabella returned she simply plopped herself down in the dinning room chair brimming over with a detailed description of her discovering of the throne room and her new friend Admiral Nelson.

The dinner Edna prepared was one of barley soup for appetizer, mutton and cabbage, creamed onions , carrots and for the main serving, and by popular demand, the three layered cake that everyone enjoyed and for Isabella came a second, smaller helping.

Edna did chide Isabella with a few more comments about her soiled dress, but let the matter subside with the resolve that she, Edna would invent a pattern of clothing for her further excursions to Toad's garden which would pretty much in the outcome make her daughter look as if she were a ceedy farm laborer.

On the following morning all three of the Tumblers, filled with the previous evening meal ate the meager remains of the barley soup, and ground their teeth on the hard crust of day old baker's bread topped of course with jams. And once finished, Isabella asked if she could be excused that she might go out into Toad's garden and crawl back into the bramble.

"You might just as well ruin those clothes for good Isabella," said Edna while she helped Isabella put on the dress she had worn the day before. "I doubt I will ever be able to scrub the dirt out, or stitch them into their original condition," said Edna resignedly as the garden doors clapped shut.

It took a bit of doing, and not without multiple more pricks of the bramble but, once she entered the hollow of the bush, Isabella began mapping a wish list for all the furnishings she would have her father build for the room and where to place each one.

The style and color of the furnishings would take time to deliberate upon but most specifically Isabella would weigh the considerations for the dimensions of her throne and where it would have the most commanding position.

Upon returning indoors for her evening bath, Isabella found in the course of telling her mother what constructions she wished Toad to build for her, Edna informed her daughter that multiple pieces of furniture were already at her disposal.

Mrs. Tumblers told Isabella that early in their marital years she had Toad construct for her a miniature Tudor mansion designed for a purpose of which Edna merely glazed over. "In the morning," Edna told Isabella "I will accompany you to the attic and we can sift through the multiple boxes that store the tiny bits of furnishings within."

Edna was overjoyed with the prospect that the dollhouse furniture which had only gained dust was finally to be used. "It was for my daughter Amaranth," she wanted to tell Isabella when asked why she had given Toad the direction to build the Tudor house and why she had furnished it to include such ornate pieces as tiny, Rococo mirrors, wall hangings woven to depict famous subjects from tapestries in the London Museum, and miniature statuary of Greco, Roman antiquities.

But Edna would not share with her Princess Daughter Isabella that she was the second princess to live in the Polstar Manor, even if the Princess Amaranth had lived but a very few years. For indeed, Edna had reasonably convinced herself that Isabella Rose was her daughter Amaranth come back to life and such an explanation was utterly useless.

Once Isabella and her mother unwrapped and dusted off each piece of furniture, Isabella chose the ones she thought would be most perfect in the space she had chosen to call: The Court of Forty. She then took the items to the bramble bush and began working at a feverish pitch to ensure everything was in a position if only temporarily.

The chandeliers were put in place first, which of course were not functioning as true light providers ; the light was to come from small wood pallets designed by Toad upon which candles were implanted, and held in place with putty and set upon the ground.

Isabella had to work through her great frustration, and even embarrassment, as she observed all the mismatch of chairs that lined the enclosed hall. How unacceptable it was that a chair designed for a dollhouse dining room set was sided with two chairs from the kitchen and those placed next to a receiving room high back, next to an overstuffed bedroom lounge chair, packed next to the ultimate in humiliation: a bench from the servant's quarters!

None the less the seating would be sufficient for the time being as Isabella concluded all of the mismatching could be coordinated to one theme once the Court was more established and she could choose an interior designer from one of her adorning subjects. For now though, Isabella knew, there was an expediency to meet her life's future adventures as the reigning monarch she was rapidly approaching .

Part Two

It had not been a fortnight when Admiral Nelson appeared again as if out of thin air and this time he was standing on his hind feet in full naval fatigues in the Court of Forty. The Admiral most assuredly noticed that Isabella had already established what might be termed a "presence" in her court and it was as if her personality could be seen and felt on every object in the room.

Admiral Nelson nodded approvingly to his potentate who was sitting on a stone she had rolled through the front entrance and then draped it with soft blue cloth and a wool pillow.

As for her appearance, Princess Isabella was clothed in the most resplendent gown sewn with her specific instructions given to Edna. The lower half of the dress was chiffon blue and had weaves of pink colored sashes, glass beads and a fanciful variety of colorful buttons none of which competed against the other. The front, top portion of the gown was a cream color with lace see-through sides, and vibrant ice green collar that flared out, up and around her head making Isabella look as if she were surrounded by a halo.

Isabella's hair was formulated this morning by her mother into a series of ringlets and long strands weaving in upon themselves; these designs Edna had perfected for herself in her days of accompanying Toad as they made imposing entrances into the stately homes of London.

"Admiral Nelson, what an unexpected surprise!" said Isabella with an edge of false bravado he could not account for.

And though Admiral Nelson was in full military attire he appeared disheveled, his tiny hairs of his body matted, his uniform torn in several places and grimy leading Isabella to perceive he had seen an abundance of warfare in the past weeks.

"My honor, Princess Isabella," said Admiral Nelson in a low, severe voice while bending ceremoniously at the waist. I must say your ascension, and your establishment of this court has not gone without notice in the animal kingdom. You have gained many loyal followers in a very few weeks; impressive to be sure," and with the sweep of his paw,

23

again, as if out of nothing the entire room of the Court of Forty had become populated with any and all variety of animal, insect and bird.

Isabella felt a small quake of surprise at such a sudden appearance of this unexpected crowd but did not allow it to show with her facial expression or bodily movement.

And to Admiral Nelson she said "I am luxuriating in these, luscious tapestry you sent ahead, Sir. The Asian motif fits remarkably well with the overall decorum; I am having fun."

"It seems we share similar tastes M'Lady," said Admiral Nelson bowing again at the waist, but this time only slightly. "I do compliment myself on being something of an accomplished horse trader and the haggling to acquire the piece you have on the south wall came with stealth maneuvering."

"I am not interested in your ability to haggle, Admiral Nelson," said Isabella tartly. "I am only interested in the application and success of your military strategies."

There was an untidy quiet in the room which hung an elongated quarter minute like improperly tuned musical notes on the clay molded chandeliers before Isabella continued: "And how is it then, on the cruel seas, Sir? The Reports coming to me Admiral have been favorable. Your successful routing of the French fleet as it rested carelessly in the Nile came with lightening precision."

Standing motionless save for his nose which never ceased twitching, Admiral Nelson responded with brief dictation showing no sign of pride or arrogance relating the account of the furious battle and his ultimate victory.

"Bravo, then!" proclaimed Princess Isabella once again in a less than sincere sounding voice. "Your rewards of success are the appreciation of all England and the celebration of our most cherished hero. Let it be recorded that among your many other posts of honor you are hereby given the title: 'Baron Nelson' ."

With this proclamation Lord Admiral Nelson, again made the slightest bow, while simultaneously putting his paw to his mouth to hide an elongated smile.

"There will be more of this," said Princess Isabella and gave leave to the populated court and to Baron Nelson encouraging him to return to his troops and carry on with all the duties engaging his new office.

Once Isabella had dismissed her subjects who strutted out rather clumsily she thought she gave herself one final moment of repose looking over her court with the presentiment that the furnishings would soon be in perfect order and then knelt down to climb upon her knees and hands out of the bramble, and out into Toad's garden.

 "If mother was cross with me earlier this week and, what a muss I have made of my appearance", considered Isabella while walking as she plucked twigs from her hair "Edna will be double-cross' with me now that my royal dress is smudged," and then laughed at the homonym she had devised.

When Isabella came up to the garden doors she found that they were slightly opened and entered the manor with nary a sound.

She could hear her parents talking in the sitting room with low barely discernible voices and moved quietly forward giving as much an ear to their private conversation as able .

"But of this royal title 'princess', my dear," said Toad to his wife, "she seems to have taken it so unhealthily far. It seems Isabella has gone about her Tom Tiddler way and is far less prepared for the world's reality than she should be by this age. I think we should at least have a plan laid out for her future; we should be consulting which girls schools are nearest."

"You Fool!" cried Edna to her husband as they sat in their chairs before the fire which was fainting slowly away. "You are daft aren't you? If I had the energy I would stuff you and hang you over the mantel. Mother always wondered at my selection of you. To think of all the handsome suitors who sniffed around for my hand in marriage! Why do I have to remind you what state of affairs we find ourselves in my husband? We do not have a plan because there can be no plan!

What?!, Isabella simply arrives on the doorstep of a school with no provable history or identification other than her name. Daft, you are."

At this moment of Toad-bashing, Edna and her husband felt the presence of another person in the room and simultaneously turned their heads to see their daughter with a strain of panic on her face.

"Isabella, please," pleaded Edna reaching out her hand "come here to me at once. There is nothing to be fearful for. Your father and I have had many a bickering-battle such as this before you came into our lives."

"What have you been saying?" said Isabella weepily. "What plan are you speaking about, what girls school? Do other girls attend school?"

Toad put his fist to his mouth and coughed out a double "harrumph" as Isabella walked gingerly to her mother's side .

"Come sit with your mother, Isabella. There's room for us both," said Edna curving her arm to embrace her daughter's waist and pulling her into the confines of her chair. "I think my girl it is time for us to have a serious chat," said Edna in a warm tone.

"Serious?" questioned Isabella.

"Yes, my child I believe it is time to be more open with you about how you have come to live here with us."

"Does this mean you will tell me I am not a real princess, Mother? Will you and Toad be sending me away from the manor...and where shall I be going....what is outside the manor mother?" said the unofficially adopted orphan child barely able to keep from crying.

"No, no, my dear, this is nothing for you to conclude. You most definitely are a princess; make no doubt about this. And no, you will never have to leave the manor as there is simply nowhere else for you to concern yourself about. Toad and I would never hear of it. No, your story, you situation is a bit more complex; more, how should we say: intriguing? More like unto a real fantasy tale."

Toad made one more of his annoying noises which earned him a determinedly angry look from Edna. Taking the clue Toad arose summarily saying he would be in his garden if he should be needed.

And when Toad had put on his garden slippers and closed the door behind him Edna began expanding into the remainder of the afternoon a tale of how Isabella had arrived at the doors of the Pulstar manor and, freely creating a tale imbuing it with atmosphere of fantastical mystery.

Edna expounded upon that auspiciously cold February afternoon when Isabella was taken in, cared for by both she and Toad, and how both of them fell so deeply in love with her that they concluded never to tell the authorities for fear she would be taken away and given, perhaps, to a wicked stepmother such as had befallen many an abandoned children: "Cinderella, for example!"

"You see my Dear," said Mrs. Tumblers in a tone that suggested she, and Toad, had done something heroic, "we cared for you because no other person would." The truth being, of course, both she and Toad would have been put on trial had the authorities discovered they had taken in an abandoned child and not reported their actions .

"You would have frozen to death out there alone with that thin blanket. You were a baby, an infant with no way of caring for yourself; without hope, and with not a soul on earth to love you. Toad and I simply had no choice."

"Then, thank you Mother, and thank you, Toad," said Isabella in a mechanical tone as she nestled her head deep into Edna's side. Isabella sat motionless, feeling very comfortable and so very safe resting against the warmth of her mother's breast, and with her hands knitting at the soft fabric of Edna's mohair sweater .

And Edna, ignoring any premise of past or present impropriety, and believing in her own invented fable, that being quite the magnanimous savior, rested her cheek affectionately onto Isabella's head.

But something was not setting right with Isabella, and in a few moments Isabella sat up with a rigid spine having concluded enough to make a statement: "Then it would seem enough to say Mother, that truly I am not a real Princess."

"But indeed you are our Princess Child," said her mother in the consoling tone.

"Oh, Isabella Rose," offered her mother "for us you are more a queen than a princess. Parents dote on their children to excess and I am sure we have been equally guilty. But then my child," said Edna snuggling her daughter even more firmly, "we do love you and I hope you will pardon us for being so naughty in not explaining everything to you sooner."

Isabella was not unused to being spoken to in such whimsical terminology and yet her spirit fidgeted within her as if she had swallowed a live guppy fish and felt it's stinging unrest as she began to comprehend that her parents had lied to her for the entirety of her life.

Isabella's hand slipped from her mother's sweater to her own side, skirted up her dress and began with her fingernails to dig deeply at her skin.

"What are you thinking," asked Edna to break the unhealthy silence which came over the room.

"Then the Polstar Manor must not be a real castle," surmised Isabella in a voice that verged on an angered accusation. "And my bedroom is not a turret overlook…"

Edna coughed lightly, putting her scarf to her mouth as if she was experiencing a painful rheumatic tremor.

"No my dear," said Edna apologetically, with a mimicked assurance, "This is hardly a castle; but, as you know, we have all the quaintness and comforts of a castle and more. I understand the early castle fortresses of say, Arthur and his men were unbearably cold, and that the men and maidens of honor went wrapped around in more animal fur than half the weight of their own bodies. Think how terribly uncomfortable life would have been; just holding your fork and knife to cut your food would have been more of an effort than killing it in the first place?"

"My dear", continued Edna, "we live in the nineteenth century; people no longer live in castles; it just isn't done, you know; we have gas heating, glass on the windows so bats won't be flying about. Can you just imagine them swooping down on you as you eat your cereal in the morning, getting caught in your hair; heavens, isn't that a frightful thought?"

"And so what are you thoughts about this my child?" asked Edna as more minutes of silence lingered on .

"Not really anything mother," lied Isabella to Edna.

Isabella sat very still in her position next to Edna digging still deeper into her bare leg until there was the breaking of skin and blood began to seep out onto the fabric of the chair. (Edna would later find this soiling of her chair and convince herself that it was nothing more than ground in soil from the garden.)

"Mother, may I go to my room now?" inquired Isabella purposely offending her mother by asking for the very freedom she had always been allowed heretofore. Isabella conjured that the dynamics of her family of three was now the configuration of two lying adults and their daughter of eleven years (if indeed she was eleven at all!) a child who would not trust any adult ever again.

"Very well, dear," said Edna stupidly, "are you not feeling well? Cricket is on the wireless soon. You know how much you love listening to Bath's team take on Scotland?"

Isabella said nothing in reply and slid from her mother's side and then walked to the hidden staircase to wend her way to the fourth floor where she closed the door of her bedroom as if she were lowering the lid upon her own coffin.

CHAPTER II

THE THREAT OF KING CRAB'

"Isabella", called Edna to her daughter as she rapped her knuckles lightly on Isabella's bedroom door . "It's almost tea time and I would like you to come and join your father and myself."

Isabella did not answer her mother as she sat propped up against the headboard of her queen sized bed waiting patiently until the bothersome noise in the hallway went away so she could turn back to her private thoughts.

To the most casual observer they would surely see Isabella's life has suddenly become difficult. Imagine for yourself that all your life you had been told your name for example is Reginald, and one day you were reading your birth certificate and found that your name was really Professor Bingo, or something insipid as this? Or, for another example, you are working a job and believe yourself to be a senior manager of a large corporation and, then someone informs you that you had just a moment before bumped your head on an overhang and that you were day-dreaming your way to greatness. How ridiculous you would feel sitting in your boss's' chair when she came into the office and began yelling at you in front of all the office employees to "get out of that seat and return immediately to the assembly line!"

This scenario of a young girl who had trusted her parents and now found they had been lying to her even before she could speak the king's language was given to Isabella who now realized she had been dethroned from her lofty position as Princess, to something of a commoner. She might just as well have been thrown from the turret window and landed in Toad's garden where she could bury her head wwith embarrassment between the potatoes and cabbage.

"Well then, who am I if I am not a Princess?" wondered Isabella not quite sure if she really cared at that point. And there, atop her bed, Isabella sat the remainder of the evening staring out blankly into her room exhausting every portion of the question while rejecting any and all answers until she eventually fell to sleep.

Isabella could not have felt more ill in her stomach, nor lost in her life's journey than when the next morning she awoke with a jolt, as if someone had poured a glass of ice water on her head.

The persistent question of whom she was hung like a damp bath cloth across her neck and she believed that her mind had not rested from the confusion all the while her body slept.

This morning, instead of tracing her outline on the dew-wet window pane, Isabella walked directly to the bathroom and rummaged in the dark for an oblong box which among several other articles held a pair of small trimming scissors. It was time, she had decided, to say goodbye to the title of Princess, and time to be born into some other role.

And it would be later in the day, when Edna again came to Isabella's door calling out and knocking, having lost all patience she placed the key into the door lock and entered the bedroom. After a second's looking for her daughter Edna walked into the bathroom and saw in the wicker trash bin a pile of shorn, mahogany-red hair.

Part II

The former Princess, Princess Isabella Rose, now merely Isabella, felt an unusual, ebullient-giddiness, an almost insane tactile connection as she made her way down her secret stairwell, undetected by her two lying parents, and crossed over the garden walk to The Court of Forty entrance.

"I must confess to you my subjects," said Isabella, as she sat upon the landing to the side of her throne weeping "that there is something of an unbelievable turn of events that has taken place ...and yet sadly it is so very true."

The entire court was filled as it were to the rafters, and in fact numerous birds and flying insects were sitting or hanging from the rafters, all concluded with certainty that their Isabella was speaking about her hair.

Everyone knew how many young ladies identified their image by the coif of their hair, and they suspected how much more a Princess would take into consideration her image being in the public eye and they were suspecting this was why she was weeping.

Indeed, their suspicions lay in the conclusion that the court hairdresser must have been absent, and that her substitute was blind in one or both eyes and cut Isabella's hair to the length a young man of their day would have worn his.

But it was to her subjects' fantastic amazement when Isabella confessed that she was standing down as their potentate.

An audible wave of disappointment rolled over those in attendance as Isabella, the former, etc, confessed, "In reality I am not a princess at all!" (Sob, sob)

Isabella Rose, controlled her sniffing that she may not burst into a flood of tears and continued by sniveling her statement, "I should in no way, in fact, I will no longer be addressing you as Subjects; rather, I am as common a human as any human, and I would like your forgiveness as we can agree to call each other simply, 'friends'".

Isabella went on to explain how she had been misled by her parents and what a breaking of her spirit this had caused her; in that she was not only crestfallen but she was utterly beside herself and wondered if anyone of them had a place where she could go to live and to work?

The deafening silence in the Court of Forty came primarily from the animal's disappointment that they were suddenly no longer members of a special Court but merely 'every day friends'.

"This is impossible!" cried out Baron Nelson. Are you are telling me that all my awards and medals, and now my title as Baron are as nothing?"

"My Dear," said Lady Emma, Baron Nelson's girlfriend who fortunately had for the first time come into the receiving hall, placed her paw upon her Baron's forearm and said "you are overreacting."

"How indeed am I overreacting?" demanded Baron Nelson facing his girlfriend with the fury of a cannon ball mshot out with the purpose of decapitating the jib sail of a frigate.

"And what are we to do?" cried Madame Praying Mantis who was standing up against the west wall behind two sightless moles who had just been engaged for marriage.

"What of the large fern plant you have granted to be exclusively that of mine and my seventy five children?" she said burying her head in her wings as praying mantis do when they wash, eat, and eh, pray.

"And of us," said Crow-Shaw the leader of Crow-Claw family clan; "are we to assume the grove of trees in County Cork are not ours alone but, to be shared with the sooty colored Festal Finch with it's incessant falsetto concert singing?"

Isabella had known what this session would bring and how devastated her friend's would be at the hearing of her abdication of her throne, but she did not account for the incredible sorrow she would feel at the idea of how she had let down all those who had come to believe and trust in her.

"Wait everyone; wait!" shouted Ms. Emma who was a strong woman activist in the community circle where she had been elected president three terms. "I will not allow any of us to stand here and accuse Princess Isabella because she has been deceived. In my mind and, of all I have heard of her from my beloved fiance', I believe Isabella to be of pure-bread Royalty for no other person or family whose court I myself have visited has there been such an unerring level of discernment and contrition as I have seen displayed in these very few minutes."

"Princess Isabella," continued Ms. Emma with a strong emphasis on Isabella's royal title

"...shall in my mind continue to reign regent as long as the Court of Forty is in existence . It is

only a matter of technical wording, and a swift vote that will allow Princess Isabella to retain her regency."

"Baron Nelson, and I," continued Lady Emma again with a strong emphasis on her man's official office, "...have come today with an urgent petition from the Grotto of the Dolphins near the coast of Sardinia."

"The Dolphin family is bound under the 'Sacred Water Bond' instituted for the protection of all sea creatures whom the greater percentage of are now in immediate peril from that which Baron Nelson will share of when he at last calms down!"

Baron Nelson gave his girlfriend Emma a stern, almost contemptuous look, but she held her gaze of adoration in the direction of Princess Isabella until Baron Nelson did indeed compose himself.

Baron Nelson then cleared his throat and bowed first to his mate Emma, and then with a more exaggerated bow at the waist, in the direction of Isabella.

"Princess Isabella", recited Lord Nelson in a respectful, and firm voice, "it is true the matter we bring to your court is of the utmost urgency, as the king of the Carthaginian Clams has

gathered to himself a hoard of the most unsavory, most despicable types from both sea, and land; from sea he has called the fearful Octagon Octopus genus who embody an electrical stingray tentacle which, as you are aware, can paralyze any creature and inflict a lifetime of suffering."

"This very same 'King of the Clams', a title he addresses himself by, has as his intent the setting of barriers across underwater ocean channels with the purpose of manipulating fish, and mammal migration."

"May I interrupt you here Baron Nelson?" asked Isabella surprising herself by using the very tone of voice that the former 'Princess' Isabella had used.

"Yes, Princess Isabella," said Lord Nelson who immediately picked up on the change in direction of conversation Isabella was referring to herself by.

"What good would it do to for the clams to interrupt the migration of fish and mammals?" "Tax purposes, M'Lady; if they are in control of the water ways they can exact taxes from any solo swimmer or school of fishes that pass in their waters. And I would suppose the King Clam has the same juvenal reason any egotist has which makes them do whatever it is that makes them egotists; if that makes any sense, M'Lady?"

"Yes, this makes perfect sense Baron Nelson. And it makes perfect sense that we put a stop to this King of Clams and his minions," charged Isabella who put her hands subconsciously to her shorn hair remembering the last time she had made as firm a decree her formerly elongated locks had whipped across her face and back which she fancied made quite a dramatic picture.

"I quite agree M'Lady," said Baron Nelson clicking his heels in full response as his epaulettes bounced on the shoulders of his uniform (thinking the action made a dramatic picture for himself as well) .

"What reconnaissance do we have on the King Clams' positioning?" asked Princess Isabella now taking full charge of the situation.

"Well, Princess Isabella," offered Baron Nelson who Emma noticed had slightly gulped when pronouncing the title: Princess, (himself somehow not one hundred percent sure everyone in the room was accepting Isabella's resurrected title) "our dolphins report concerning the King Clam forces , and where they will make their very first assault, reveal their activities will be the Eastern water way to the Indian ocean from the undersea channel known as the Careful Channel."

"He has at his resources the occupi to lead the charge, and sea horses that we would all agree are adorable in appearance , but who have given their cuteness to the "unhappy side" of life. There is also a band of killer whales that claim they are out to make their names even more feared; and then as I have reported there are any number of smaller fishes whom Clam's words and promises have seduced."

"Then in no small way has this arrogant muscle, by the calling together of troops, declared war; do you not agree Baron Nelson?"

"I am in total agreement M'Lady."

"And our forces, Baron Nelson?" inquired Isabella who knew that as her imagination had convened the Court of Forty and ,all of the characters who were there in her own fairy tale, she could just as well imagine a navy large enough for Baron Nelson to command and defeat the Clam King.

"Your navy is at the ready to serve you as myself am Princess Isabella; we await your orders."

Suddenly there came an invisible force of mutual understanding and acceptance that blew around the room as if a fog of grief and mystery spewed out of a wicked witch's broom tail making it impossible for anyone present to move.

But it was Lady Emma who found the ability to speak and once her jaw moved it felt to her as if she were breaking herself free of a clay molding.

"I think the issue here is that we are all at Princess Isabella's service but and unless we witness an official coronation we will be unable to perform those services. My suggestion is that in keeping with the traditions and the justices of our lands, that in the absence of the Queen of the British Isles, and in the urgency of this impending war, we ourselves officiate the proceedings."

"We will of course, in time, have to defer this alfresco coronation to an official adjudicator, but for now . .. " And here Lady Emma's voice trailed off as she deferred the remainder of her suggestion to her Baron.

"It is so in the time of extreme circumstances," continued Baron Nelson "that we with all deference to our Queen and the legalities of our beloved land we initiate this proceeding. For I agree that in the days to come we will have an official adjudicator officiate the decisions we make here, which will probably amount to no more than an arcane desk clerk punching a seal onto an unreadable document. Expediency, I say, is our purpose and we must not falter!" championed Baron Nelson with a pounding of one fisted paw into the open palm of the other.

When Nelson had finished with his statement, and given pause, the room engaged like so many English proceedings, in a polite placing together of whatever appendices would account for each being's ability to clap with approval.

Baron Nelson, and not until the clapping ceased, clicked his heels and removed his silver tipped sword from its scabbard, lifting his arm at a right angle.

"This can't be real," thought Isabella putting her fingertips up under her clothing feeling for the cut she had given to herself on her leg.

"And yet it is real; the Court of Forty is a real place. It may be in the hollowed out portion of the sweetbriar but all the same I am a Princess. I know I am a Royal Princess!"

Isabella, as if moving from a dress rehearsal into a first time live stage production moved from her crouching position and slithered snail like down the three steps where she landed more or less in a sitting position in the center of the ornate receiving carpet which had arrived only days earlier as a gift from the Sultan of Persia.

There Isabella balanced up to a kneeling position as Baron Nelson, once again clicking his heels, stepped forward, his sword at the ready, lay it down on Isabella's right then left shoulder as gently as a silken snowflake falls on a kitten's nose and then back again to her right once again lifting it to a right angle and proclaiming:

"In her Majesty's absence," (Baron Nelson's voice resonating like the beginning movement of a grand orchestra piece) , "and to the great delight of all the citizenry of the land of Great Britain; it's soaring reputation that reaches to the ends of all the planet, capturing the hearts, hopes and dreams ...".

Baron Nelson was apt to go on, and on, when deliberating publicly at events where he had a captive audience. Lady Emma knew that any person or creature of any size or shape with ears to hear; who was forced to sit through an elongated speech would soon be drifting off thinking about raisin pudding, raisin pudding topped with worms, in the case of the birds.

Lady Emma had fashioned a code of communication both visual and nasal that began as a twirling of her fan between her paws and long, modulated sighs.

This "twirling" did not go unnoticed by the Baron, nor the sighs which tended to be longer, and louder the more he ambled on. In response Baron Nelson took the hint and curtailed his commencement declarations to only a few sentences more.

"Rise Princess Isabella," said Baron Nelson as he lifted his sword higher into the air pointing the blade towards the apex of the nave where two female bats, who were weeping with joy, and whose tears trickled down upo Lady Skunk's new hat, "...let all of Brittan know the name, Rose, Isabella Rose, is hereby ordained Princess for life!"

Isabella Rose, rose from her kneeling position, not realizing she was humming the tune to 'God Save the Queen' !

Now, an official Princess, Isabella, returned to her official throne, and faced her 'official' subjects, with a firm but kind gaze. "I believe Baron Nelson, spoke Isabella with her chin angled upwards "the subject was about our readiness for war?"

"And indeed we are M'Lady though the plans for our counter offense will take some time to deliberate upon. May I suggest, my Princess, you attend our war room meeting which I have taken the liberty to schedule tomorrow at eight AM sharp ."

"Eight o'clock then, Baron Nelson, and with your approval I would like to open that convocation to everyone in this room seeing as how it will involve all of their lives in one way or another ."

"Excellent notion Princess Isabella," responded Baron Nelson.

"Eight o'clock! " commanded Isabella as she stood from her throne and her subjects; insect, fowl, and mammal, bowed with great courtesy and regard. Not another word was spoken as her Highness found her way to the door and appeared at the border of Toad's garden on her knees, and hands once again all a muss but this time a true princess.

Part III

Later in the day at high tea, Edna glared angrily towards Toad as he tried over and over to begin to make reference to Isabella's hair and, with every attempt, she curtailed his speech with interruption.

In her youth Edna was something of a rebellious sort, purposely dressing out of fashion, not completing her school studies, and staying at her friend's houses late into the night so that her parents would rock with grief wondering if their daughter had been run over by a trolley.

"Isabella is simply going through one of her stages," said Edna with a sniff of disdain, irritated that she, once again, had to explain everything to the 'Toadster' about female "anything!".

But of course Edna was concerned for her daughter as it was not only the hair in the trash that was disturbing; this would have been nothing horribly wrong. But it was the gloomy silence with which Isabella carried about her as if it were a visible mantle of grief replacing her formerly long hair.

For the first time in the Tumbler family domestics, Isabella began to mimic the general dull, day-to-day movements within the manor which became all to obvious as heretofore Isabella's actions and activities were synonymous with that of an adorable pixie fairy who flitted about with the wonderment of a curious child.

Like Toad, and Edna, Isabella now began to rise pretty much the same quarter hour as they, washing and primping herself before going down to the kitchen to help with the setting of the breakfast, letting her mother be 'mother' taking a 'cuppa', and often clearing the cups and saucers once Toad and Edna confined themselves to their parlor seats.

Isabella commandeered a stuffed chair, (a poor princess throne as she called it) one she had notice in a side room of the manor and instructed Toad to clean it and set it with his and Edna's.

And as they sat that first evening, the three of them together, but actually apart, (as Isabella would no longer sit in the same chair or on the sofa with either of her parents) Isabella concluded that she rather enjoyed devising ways to upset the prescribed tedium of this untrustworthy couple.

In the mornings for example, Isabella rushed to beat Toad into the parlor, took control of the wireless, and set the station for the children's performance shows which she would not allow him to adjust.

There was no end to her pranks; whether it was the tying of Toad's bathrobe arms into one of the many sailor knot designs taught to her by Baron Nelson's midshipman, or using one of her mother's favorite tea cups as a planter for a small flower.

With several weeks of these goings-on Toad who had worked in the banking business for all his career and had ingested a sure summation of many difficult lessons by encountering the many moods and temperaments of both client and employer, earned a reputation for sidestepping angry, or tense confrontations with these people by showing an attitude of quiet grace, and overreaching humility.

But when it came to the radio in his own domicile, the temptations of Isabella's impishness proved too much for the poor old man, and gave cause to his storming out to his garden on several occasions in his stocking feet.

"Who ever this child was," he would say to himself as the damp of the ground began to penetrate his socks "she has situated herself to be more of a bother than a gift."

And it was not as if Edna was unawares of the trouble that was beginning to brew on the back porch of the Pulstar Manor with the roses Toad had successfully potted every year from eternity past, the all but impossible to invigorate Centifolia Rose, had recently died due to some unknown rotting of the roots for which there was no real explanation save that someone had purposely poured something poisonous onto them. (But whom?)

"Even if Isabella is responsible my husband" said Edna to Toad as she massaged his shoulders while he leaned forward in the high back, his elbows on his knees, his face cupped on the fists of his hand "we know that it was due to the sudden change in her character."

"Then my wife... ," said Toad, his words barely discernible in that his fists gave little movement for the jaw to open effectively. "We must consult a doctor of the emotions. It cannot be that we can go on allowing her to assault the serenity of this our home with pranks that amount to all out vandalism!"

("The 'serenity of our home' thought Edna. 'Serenity' more properly spelled would be: b-o-r-e-d-o•m.")

Edna remonstrated once again: "There is no way in Tumblr Wells Down! How on earth do we explain Isabella to the authorities? Haven't we been through this one thousand times before? Aren't we in perfect agreement that the authorities would give no quarter, though the evidence is more than sufficient that God, by His infinite mercies, gave us back our baby girl, and that we …, We should thank God that she has not become sufficiently ill that we have had to contact a medical doctor. What then my husband? What then?"

Toad only nodded the way husbands do to whatever their wives are trying to reason their position on a subject when all the while they are resolute in their own conclusions. Better the woman save her energies and spend them picking up the scattered pieces of man's fractured follies than to believe they have changed his mind.

And so the battle for the dominion of Pulstar Manor would be met head-on, reasoned Toad. What had happened to the adoring child whom had adhered to every wish of her parents with strict obedience; one who listened to each word as if it were some ancient verse for human survival carved in the sides of Stonehenge; a child who sat rapt with attention as Toad enhanced the figures of fables and children's literature with great delight, even all out laughter for allowing himself the freedom he could never have enjoyed while being a "pillar of the community?"

True, the story readings with Isabella gave him an opportunity to become the stage performer he had always dreamt of being when he was in the grade schools. "Promising future", his sixth grade teacher had told him when he performed in an abridged production of Chaucer's Canterbury Tales.

But the stage was not for he, his father had told him so. "Securities", emphasized his father as the small but abusive man rapt his steel-like fist on the dining table of their home when Toad presented him the outline for a thespian's successful future.

Sadly though, Toad had to admit to himself, there is no gain anguishing over the past. He

had not amassed his financial empire by writing poetic sonnets about lost empires or lost loves.

It was Edna who wanted the child she would come to call Amaranth and cried until Toad had given in. "But you will be the one to raise this child," he had warned his wife; "my duties are that of the provider." And this she agreed upon with such satisfaction that she literally dropped to her knees and kissed Toad's Savile Row shoes.

It was not long after the Amaranth' s birth that Toad, despite the rigidity of his personality and the demands of his banking securities schedule that he found himself coming home from work every day at least one hour early hoping to have a few moments to play with Amaranth on the carpet and letting her ride on his back as he made ridiculous horse noises.

But these joys were short lived as it was a nurse from the hospital who called directly upon Toad while he sat in the bank board room maneuvering over charts and balances with his staff, and forced to listen about his need to hurry home.

"Never again, resolved Toad would he allow his guard to come completely down, which in the context of the so-called: "Return of Amaranth" would his emotions of care or concern be given to such great degree that he might not now pull them easily back.

Had Isabella acted in strict, discipline manners, then all would be well and he, Toad, would hold her close enough to protect, and nurture her for the remainder of his days. "But, Toad said to himself condescendingly, "Isabella has chosen a different path; never mind her mother's excuses about Isabella being youthful and full of excessive, childish energy . The matter was one of civility; indomitable fortifications of 'rights ' and 'wrongs' were the rules he lived by, not languid promises meant to be stretched every which way.

Toad resolved to continue acting his part in the drama that worked as if it had been written for the complete upending of the Pulstar Manor . But alas, he would alter the script; edit it to his very liking. His character which seems to have been cast as the benign, 'Fatuous Father', would now be written as the 'Wretched Papa' .

Surely in regards to his 'adopted' daughter his business would be to crush the demon spirit that had seeped into this quiet retirement life.

Who knows what curse may have been cast upon Isabella when she was first born? Her birth mother could well have been a real Gipsy for all they knew. Perhaps this foreign mother was a member of a mystic society and the spell she had conjured for the girl-child was that Isabella would come to he and Edna as a sort of Trojan Horse?

"Crush the Demon spirit," said Toad with resolve whispering it as if in meditation. "Break its neck; kill it in the nest. Life will be normal at the Manor again; safe, normal, and absolutely free of Isabella Rose!"

Chapter III

THROUGH THE BRAMBLE BUSH'

(... and what Isabella found there.)

The air was tense when Isabella crawled back through the bramble and approached the entrance portico of the Court of Forty now secured by two large black crows . The crows stood rigid as stones, each having highly polished, sharpened beaks, and stern, attentive looks in their black eyes .

"Good afternoon Princess Isabella," said the one on the right as the bird on the left pushed open an imaginary set of oak double doors.

"Good afternoon Soldiers of the Crow family," said Isabella nodding politely and then focused her attention upon her throne where she would begin business immediately.

All heads bowed as Isabella made her way to the end of the hall and took favorable notice that every being in the room was dressed in battle fatigue, most notably Lady Emma whom, never without a hat, wore a navel headdress usually designated for second-in-commands of

English vessels. The only difference was, Lady Emma had fastened a great plume of a falcon feather into the ridge of the head strap and had died it with a garish purple.

And if this captured the attention of those in the court, it was Baron Nelson who dressed in the most flamboyant of coats, and he, wearing the traditional sea commanders headdress, also had a plume of an eagle's feather placed in his head band and this given him by Eagleson Tremors), the leader of the eagle spy, reconnaissance team whose territory covered the length of the British Isles and across the channel into many parts of Northern Europe.

"Please," said Isabella in a calming tone "We are certainly all of one heart as we approach this battle, and I wish to make it abundantly clear that anyone of you who may have second thoughts about the actual fighting I assure you we support you in your decision, and there is no shame.

No beast, insect or bird of prey expected any of the subjects gathered to move a hood, pincer, or claw in the direction of the exit door, and none were disappointed.

After only a few moments Isabella spoke again; "We shall now hear from Baron Nelson who will inform us of our final orders."

"M'Lady," said Baron Nelson who bowed briskly in the direction of his Princess but catching a shifting of emotion in the room. He looked quickly around to see a number of his sailors smiling, and even chuckling while they pretended to not look at him, but did anyway.

Baron Nelson glanced towards Lady Emma with a "What's the matter?" look in his eyes when she communicated back indicating that a part of the purple plume from her hat had dislodged from its holding and was now clinging to his shoulder .

Baron Nelson's eyes flashed with embarrassment, as he quickly shot his paw up and brushed the peacock-like adornment off . He then took in a deep breath and began his briefing, the instruction of which consisted of the formation of the attack boats and the flight of the numerous lookout birds who would gage the currents and waves via the winds.

The pelicans in particular would be estimating the depth of potential hazards such as jagged coral beds or if the waters ahead were mined with floating explosives . There was also new information that Baron Nelson could not help but be impressed with and made a showing of it with his voice that picked up rapidly .

For this pronouncement Baron Nelson cleared his voice to show that he wanted to give an outstanding proclamation. "With providential fortune Princess Isabella, word of our battle with King Crab has reached the ears of Svetlana the Good Queen of the Seals and she has decided that she will grant you an audience with her that she may impart some pertinent information to you."

Princess Isabella the adroit leader she was, knew enough not to show a change of affections when given news of such importance, but rather to nod her head as if in a meditative state pondering all of the dimensions and possible consequences.

And when she did speak, she again made no sign of enthusiasm that she may reassure her subjects that with bad or in this case good fortune all would continue on a steady course.

"What would you suggest an appropriate gift for Queen Svetlana?" inquired Princess Isabella raising her voice with sufficient queries in that all subjects present may give their imaginations to the topic .

"May I suggest M'Lady," said Count Featherun of the Tribe of Pelicans "something that would challenge her intellect; say a puzzle for instance?"

"May I inquire Count Featherun why something in the form of a quiz for a present? Might we not take a chance on offending Queen Svetlana, suggesting perhaps, unintentionally of course , that we wish to best her intelligence by seeking her failure at something?"

"Quite the contrary Princess Isabella; in an over flight across her mysterious island several years ago, Rasputininsky, one of my soldiers, observed a visitor to her island who presented Queen Svetlana with a small, but intricately carved box."

"My soldier, not knowing if he were disturbing a portion of a private island ritual sat hidden on a tree branch bearing the encumbrance of ants climbing onto his legs while he made his observation . He then saw Queen Svetlana take many moments to examine the box. She then with the flick of one of her fingers on a hidden latch which caused the box open . And inside there was revealed a precious stone ring of which, my soldier being uneducated in gemology did not have a name. He says Queen Svetlana was immensely pleased with herself having figured the riddle and placed the ring immediately onto to a flipper with its leathery adjustable band waving it wildly to her mermaid servants."

"Then we shall have a challenge as a gift for her Highness of the Mermaids," said Isabella and pondered what to choose for her while looking to the ceiling in the same manner as if someone were searching for a full, ripe apple .

"May I put forth a notion?" queried David Stumpfh, a portly porcupine with rosy cheeks that looked as though he had stuffed small apples with. Isabella nodded in affirmation and David Stumpfh began to illiterate.

"I once saw a trick performed M'Lady when a band of Gypsies came round Liverpool where I was living with my second wife; my first wife Heather having passed away due to an infection received in a fall. . .the doctors were baffled altogether. .. arguing among themselves ... I was in a position to as I was standing behind a curtained barrier..."

David Stumpfh seemed capable of extending a conversation to the point where even Baron

Nelson would begin fidgeting and was reprimanded by one of the Tribe of Turtle members who inadvertently belched which caused Mr. Stumpfh to realize what he was doing and he stopped.

As David paused, Isabella smiled delightfully so that any embarrassment Mr. Stumpfh might take was rather turned to a fun scenario even as the rhythm of war drums beat.

David completed the telling of the Gypsy trick which amounted to small, floating sticks in a basin of water and given a particular command, would dance on the surface of the water like fanciful ice skaters.

"And you have knowledge of this command?" inquired Princess Isabella.

"I do indeed, M'Lady," said Mr. Stumpfh proudly. "It all begins. ." Mr. Stumpfh, the portly Mr. Stumpfh, now reveling in the light of everyone's attention having been cast upon him, shifted himself to a position to dialog, a loooooooong explanation of how he had intercepted the magic command whereby Isabella interjected again saying she was sure Mr. Stumpfh was indeed capable of initiating the trick, thanked him for sharing the remainder of his information by placing it into a sealed report, and went briskly to the subject of sea vessels, readiness of troops, and numerous other questions she would ask of Baron Nelson or those most qualified to answer them.

Unfortunately, for all those in attendance, the strategies for implementing a counter offensive against the King Crab piled upon itself excessive hours in the Court of Forty.

Isabella in expectation of this, and other meetings to follow, had assembled enough chairs to seat her fellow country attendees, constructed perches for fowls, stored food, and drink to be serviced from the kitchen, and had the foresight to include multiple jars of mites, spiders, and pill-bugs for the crows, and other fowl to eat.

When all syllables and words from all the participant's mouths were as soldiers in one straight line, all motions motioned, and votes cast and counted, Isabella championed the delegation of multiple interests, by adjourning the meeting.

Toad was tilling the garden when Isabella emerged from the bush. There was no greeting by Toad who did his very best to ignore his child .

Isabella did her best to maneuver around Toad and his activities. "I'll have that lad out of here," muttered Toad to himself watching Isabella with her shorn hair in her rogue clothes walking nimbly to the manor.

Isabella entered the sitting room and hastened to the manors' central stairwell. For jest she liked to imagine herself a large slithering iguana as she walked upwards, and hugged the staircase banisters leaning her body close and sticking out her tongue with quick flashes while making piercing hissing sounds.

"And do you see how she goes up and down the staircase? cursed Toad to his wife "A fine young lady would never do such a thing," he said while combing his fingers along his scalp. "Gypsies, I say. They were the ones left that creature on our doorstep."

"My, we are in a fanciful mood of discontent, are we not Mr. Toad?"

Toad turned to his wife already acknowledging to himself that she was not one to be won over to his side of angst. Nonetheless he had no other person to rant to; it was not as if he could pop down to the pub and complain to his cronies.

"You have one look at her skin color my Dear; this should be convincing even to the most ardent worshiper," he said losing a great deal of pent up tension with the wind he blew through his nostrils. "She is assuredly no daughter of England; she is a Gypsy I say: a bewitched Gypsy."

Isabella did not bother to take a shower when she entered her room. Rather she propped her bottom up to the back of her bed headboard and allowed the dirt of the Court of Forty to shake out where it may give a new, soiled coloring to the theretofore-lavender bed spread.

There was much to contemplate. Truly and for always Isabella knew she would reign as Princess, and neither Mother, nor Toad, could ever again take the title away from her.

There was to be war with no telling how much destruction of body and property she and her subjects would have to endure. It would be necessary for Isabella to lead the faithful and she would take the responsibility if her fighting armada were not successful.

Obviously Isabella would stand in the dangerous position alongside Baron Nelson on the main deck and not Lady Emma who had requested as much. Instead, Lady Emma would wait in the womb of the ship. Indeed, there was no use her taking in the shock of a battle considering she was with child; perhaps many a child.

This coming battle against an idiotic, egocentric crab would be one grand adventure! There would be the excitement of hearing the roar of cannon every bit as intense as illustrated in the books about Pirates; with all of the frothy smoke, and smell of gunpowder combusting to kick large steel balls through cribbage parlors in homes for the retired and infirmed. Birds were certain to screech their great ranting, calling forward the battleships and guiding the projectiles of attack-ship mortar fire to their targets so true.

Watchful dolphins would accompany the convoy popping up out of the water and diving back as if they were rhymes written with silver skin.

The evil octopus clan would have to be fought differently than any other sea dweller. Octopi had the reputation of laying in wait among rocks or on the seafloor with their attack tentacles ready to strike like lightening bolts, disrupting entire schools of fish that were out on fish picnics nibbling on algae or playing fishy hide-and-seek among the crevices of coral .

Depth charges might dislodge the nasty ocupi or razor sharp arrows shot from flinger guns by those rabbits who had volunteered to put on diving suits and swim into the treacherous, murky waters.

Isabella's troops would fly the victory flag, she was for the most part certain and, indeed from this point forward she would not allow herself to think of anything other than complete victory.

And right there on the deck of her carrier vessel, up for all to see, Isabella saw herself decorating Baron Nelson, and all those who served in the battle, one-by-one, with sterling medals and opulent sashes with the Court of Forty insignia, a capital 'I' for Isabella , woven onto them.

Isabella sat and thought of this potentially grand adventure until she sunk down into her sheets and began walking herself down the lane which leads to slumber land; a dimly lit lane where loose gravel crunched under her shoes and after numberless steps dissolved, Isabella was caught floating up aimlessly among the immense trees full of crisp leaves and small fruits with their juicy flavors, but no pits to worry about which could potentially get caught in her throat.

If you could see Isabella's face at this time, even with her beautifully chiseled face caked upon by tiny splotches of mud, you would not see the face of a child whom at one time was dethroned from her position of princess and now had gained it back with more rule of authority; instead, you would see streaks of terror that tried demolishing each other as angry neighbor dogs try biting at you through openings in a fence.

What whips of fear had crashed down upon the orphan's soul, when she who knew none of the things of this world, a singularly helpless creature who lay pray to that which pried her away from the comfort of her real mother's arms; had she been abandoned like rubbish from the morning breakfast, most likely not; she had been placed in a basket and wrapped in warm blankets, surely there was someone whom had cared for her?

But where was this person? Did she only have a birth mother, or did she also have a father brothers and sisters too?

Great, dark forms loomed in her memory; shapes an infant would have no language for. And these shapes that came down around her were in reality the shapes of horse hooves.

There were also shocking waves of bright orange and red color; fire and wafts of smoke which carried sprinkling cinders of wood from homes of the village Isabella was born in.

And those screams! From horses, from the men who were crushed by them or riddled through with bullets and knife blades and the women, mothers crying out for themselves and their lost children.

Isabella slept a torturous few hours before she was awaken by trumpets and drums commanding a call-to-arms. There was also a call to breakfast by you-know-who but of whom Isabella ignored as she brushed at her hair with her hand like the upstair maid spanking an old mattress. She did not bother to go into the bathroom wash her face or rinse her mouth, and instead simply carried her dignified being down the multiple stairs and out to the garden to the doors to the Court of Forty.

And this time there were not just two guards but a quartet whom all in unison bowed deep their heads into their chests with the Captain saying "All hail Princess Isabella, benevolent, wise leader of her subjects."

"All hail! came another call as Isabella came through the doors and into the grand expanse of the Court with every inch of it's multiple mosaic floor designs covered with the feet, paws, hooves, and constricted razor sharp claws of anxious souls turned out for the duties of soldering.

"And to you my faithful subjects," shouted Isabella Rose as she climbed the steps to her throne, not sitting but wanting to make eye contact with each upturned face.

"I am," she began "as you are to me, undyingly at your service for a cause that transcends all of our singular needs and wants, and for the good and security of the whole, we shall fight until there is no more thing of evil to fight, and this is our purpose, our goal and our pledge!"

Thus shouting out these stirring words the Court of Forty exploded with the cheers of Isabella's subjects, the noise of which rose to the ceiling chandeliers shaking them as if an earthquake had moved the foundations of the building .

Part II : The Intrepid

"We are on course, Princess Isabella," shouted Baron Nelson to his Sovereign, overcoming the high winds of the Mediterranean which threw angry wafts of air like invisible pillows into his face and sent swirls of salt into his furry ears.

"And Lady Emma?" returned Isabella to the indomitable profile of Baron Nelson who stood like a flint.

"I had my First Lieutenant look in on her last hour," said Lord Nelson. "She is wanting for nothing, and as I suspected had dictated her answer from a kneeling position by her bed. She is uncommonly religious," he said as the whiskers on his nose twitched a bit too vigorously thought Isabella.

"We shall be well then M'Lady; the sea is rough as expected in this winter season. The dolphins report no depth charges in our path, no floating mines, no nets with spikes to ground our ships, but we shall not offend our own wisdom by thinking the enemy is ignorant of our approach."

The stinging waters continued throwing their misty might upon the decks of the Intrepid which was the name of the Baron's vessel; a brisk, sleek mid-sized craft with a mere eighteen guns in its belly. The craft was not designed as a full-on attack ship, rather, one which could maneuver close to large warships, fire gaping holes into their water lines, and then hopefully escaping before being hit themselves.

The voyage would take an approximate fourteen days from the port of Liverpool, through the Straits of Gibraltar, and then around to the coast of Sardinia where they would encounter the King Clam stronghold. For Isabella Rose this turned into little more than several seconds of dreaming before she felt it was time the fairy tale would be enhanced by the encounter with the Queen of Seals.

The Intrepid had come to more gentle waters by the time evening tea was served and was floating under a full moon as it passed the last markings of the country France when Baron Nelson said "M'Lady . .. "

"Baron Nelson," interrupted Princess Isabella "it is your message from the Commander of the whales of which you will address me; is it not?"

"Yes, M'Lady, answered Baron Nelson.

"And that which you have to report to me is something causing you great consternation, said Isabella as she simultaneously blew upon her spoon which held a wonderfully blended bisque the chef had prepared.

"Begging your pardon M'Lady but it is not so much the word 'consternation' which defines the message of the whales; rather it is the mystery if I may term it this way that gives me pause.

"These are times of war Baron Nelson; I should guess that you are not unused to mysteries?"

"This is true M'Lady and then, peradventure allow me to report there seems to be a very-queen of the seals! It is true; that which has been unsubstantiated and thought to have been little more than a sailor's myth, that seals will communicate with humans!"

"And of them Baron Nelson, and indeed for whatever purpose does the Commander of the whales bring you news of this?

"She, the Queen, does indeed request a visitation from us, M'Lady. And if I am to interpret the tone to which Commander Orca dictated the message, the request is more like a demand. It seems the Mediterranean Ocean is the domain she considers to be personally hers. With due regards Mum", said Baron Nelson with a slight bow of the head a position he had not calculated would place the tips of his whiskers into his soup bowl.

"I see", said Princess Isabella with a tart raise to her voice. "Then if this is her domain, continued Isabella in a way that competing women take up defense against each other's wiles "then I suppose we the lowly travelers must take time out of this expedition to pay court to One-so-grand as she."

"Indeed we must Princess Isabella," said the tiny bunny whose dampened whiskers were being attended to by his devoted significant-other-bunny. "She has baited us in saying she has knowledge of a weakness of the King Clam's which she is considering imparting to us if only we pay homage."

"Sounds more than just a little vain," said Lady Emma keeping her voice low as bunnies do when not wanting to interrupt conversation but none the less saying it just loud enough so as not to be unheard.

"Sounds as if this might be a fair enough evaluation," said Isabella grinning towards Emma who was continuing to dry Baron Nelson's whiskers just for the sake of showing him that even a Baron must take care for the smaller things in life.

"Then we shall change course Baron Nelson that we may pay respects to this Queen of the Mediterranean, a lady whom seems to take pride in possessing what is most certainly not the only file in her bureau drawer of social vicissitudes."

At this point the Intrepid came up to the Straits of Gibraltar which have been known to keep ships as it were in limbo, with strong currents rushing one way and intense winds blowing in the opposite direction. Once through the Straits there would be a direct route to the island Ibiza and somewhere along this path the Queen would send an entourage to meet the Intrepids visitors and guide them to her secret fortress.

To help the Intrepid carve its way through the Mediterranean water which rushed like race horses to the Atlantic Ocean, two whales, one at starboard the other port side, nudged the Intrepid forward with their noses as if the ship were an oblong glob of pea soup straining through a sieve.

Of the two giants the mammal on the starboard side sought an introduction with Isabella and this was Christina, a baleen whale whose skin when breaching the water and reflecting the sun looked as if she were made of highly polished steel.

The Intrepid was well under its own sailing power by this time and Princess Isabella watched over the bulwark as a fine male cormorant named Trevor lighted on the railing with her and translated a conversation started between Isabella and Christina.

Princess Isabella, with her inquisitive mind was not one to ask typical questions one would expect a human to inquire of a Baleen. Her's were questions young women ask their peers; questions of vanity, travel, journeys, and famous personalities the whale may have encountered, and of course about young men whales, or dreams of young men, and how Christina, being young by whale standards, was just as Isabella, seeking a Prince worthy of all her heart's longings.

Trevor flinched at this girlish interchange of passions finding them more distasteful than having swallowed a bottom-sucker scavenger fish.

Isabella knew there was time enough before they reached the Queen's to continue the banter with Christina, before eventually turning attention to the several questions she had in reference to The Queen of the Seals and what it was like living in her domain?

"I quite understand your thoughts of the Mediterranean Seas being a bit too grand for one to take dominion over," said Christina who understood the emphasis Isabella had placed on the possessive pronoun "her".

Christina related the Queen had not taken the property rights by virtue of arrogant domain instead she had inherited her position from her mother. "Her mother died, my Princess friend, from wounds inflicted by a harpoon cast at her from a Phoenician sailors sailing boat about four thousand years ago."

"The daughter watched as the men pulled her mother onto their deck, mocked her, and then hacked her to pieces with axes."

"I see," said Isabella sorrowfully. "How terribly awful; it is surprising she wishes to see me considering I am human."

"Indeed you will be the first human the Queen has ever granted an audience."

Isabella found her shoulders had begun to sag with the weight of such an unpleasant story and then straightened her spine by pulling back her shoulders, and taking a deep breath said, "We are very much prepared for our meeting with the Queen; one of our Court members suggested we bring the Queen Seal a gift of intrigue and challenge."

"You have been well informed to do this, your Highness , and yes , it is true the Seal Queen loves any chance to match her wits against problems." Suddenly Christina's attention was captured by a shimmering school of minnows and gave a brief salutation before diving down with the intention of swallowing them whole .

Isabella thanked Trevor for his interpreting the conversation between herself and Christina and left the deck of the Intrepid not quite sure about something that was ruminating deep within her subconscious .

Isabella ascended the stairs to go to her state room recognizing with a nod to the guard Seraphine Serpent a potentially deadly coral snake that was never not coiled on her doorstep ready to strike at any unwelcome intruder.

Isabella spent her evening on her bed with her knees propped under her chin taking in and letting out modulated breaths which set her into a state of self improvised hypnotization .

In both a logical sense, as well as a metaphorical sense, Isabella was in very deep waters . It is one thing to embark on a journey, say for example packing your knapsack with a jelly and butter sandwich, an apple, and a something to drink, and then go along to the city zoo for a day's encounter with animals who live behind bars, and otters, or seals who swim to the delight of the human eye behind the security of an enclosure.

But it is something else again to walk, or in this case float into the midst of the animal king•and-Queendoms, with no guaranteed protection for your physical well being.

"Four thousand years," said Isabella in a meditative breath that would linger in an unhappy picture before her face as if it were a puff of cigar smoke had formed into a condemning, clenched fist with an index finger pointed out to her. Somehow this imposing fist was able to speak to

Isabella and began accusing her by saying "What harmful games are you playing with nature's children?"

"What indeed have we done to our human children?" said Isabella Rose who strangely enough found herself in dialogue with a cloudy fist .

Yes, Isabella was not ignorant of the human world that teemed with misery just beyond the gates of Pulstar Manor. Often times when Edna and Toad thought she was in her room asleep, or in the back yard fondling the textures of flowers, Isabella had hidden behind the den curtains to listen to the radio news about the horrible wars being fought with teargas and bayonet's on Europe's main-lands.

There were also stories coming from hospital emergency rooms where children had been treated having been burned on their fingers with cigarettes by their parents to show them what hell would feel like if they showed disobedience to their school masters.

There was also the elongated conversation between Toad and a visitor at their front door; a slow speaking man, Inspector D....... Inspector D .... was making inquiries about the murder

of an unidentified person found on the far side of the footbridge next to the place where Edna took up her mail each morning.

Assuredly, there was something not right with the dual worlds' she was living in and, yet somehow, Isabella had no difficulty moving into one and out of the other with simple ease.

And just at the depths of these ruminations, seconds before the particular wolves she had conjured for this ocean going world were inches from biting her, Isabella concluded she must end this nonsensical play-dream of leading so many innocent creatures into war, Lady Emma, having been given Seraphine's permission, began beating furiously on her state room door, and shouting about Isabella's need to come quickly to the bridge!

Only Lady Emma, who possessed the power of personality, coupled with sensitivity, could have pulled Princess Isabella out of her melancholia and talked to her as she took her Princess by the hand, leading her to the Intrepid's bridge where Baron Nelson stood looking out his spyglass.

Lady Emma turned and walked to the hatch that led to her lover-Baron's small library, while Nelson handed the spyglass to Isabella and pointed in a Southeastern direction to a black mobile object becoming larger as it approached their ship.

"The King Clam's Navy?" questioned Isabella to her Baron? "No , My Ladyship, this is a transport vessel to take you to The Queen of the Seals."

As it came into greater focus Isabella strained her eyes, while Baron Nelson commented upon the twin, sleek porpoise who were bounding through the water leading something that can be best described as a giant glass bubble resting atop the back of sea tortoise.

Also sitting atop the tortoise shell, were two mermaids who appeared to be in the process of guiding the transport and whose long hair stands were caught up in the wind and billowed out like oversized, beach blankets.

"The fowls have told me Your Ladyship," said Baron Nelson who was looking over the bulwark as the tortoise shell came up alongside the Intrepid, "that the glass bubble atop our tortoise taxi is our carriage and that we should have no concern about it dislodging. They have also informed me that the door to the bell-jar is not so perfectly secure and may let in a few specks of water droplets. "

Isabella and Baron Nelson made their way down the ship ladder to the boarding platform and stood waiting for either of the mermaids' instruction to come aboard the turtle . The dolphins, who in their playful way, were taking turns bounding out of the water to see which of them could with its nose touch the mast head, came crashing back down to the water and accidentally or not splashed the Princess and the Baron who learned the certainty of how frigid the sea waters were.

"Will Lady Emma be traveling with us?" asked Princess Isabella with a hopeful tenor in her voice as she stood almost gasping for air, her breath having all but left her mute with the sudden shock of cold .

"I think it not prudent M'Lady;" said Baron Nelson not unused to being as it were slapped with frozen salt "in Lady Emma's state of pregnancy that she travel with us; the churning effects of the ocean waves may be more than she is physically able to endure."

But Lady Emma would prevail against such cautions from her man and, made the decision to go as well.

The two mermaids, one with a silvery dark blue tint to her skin and red angry eyes , and the other with deep black skin and equal hatred in her violet eyes, waved Princess Isabella, Baron Nelson, and Lady Emma from the boarding platform and up the simple steps into the glass jar.

The two mermaids in unison screamed like child banshees commanding the dolphins to begin the journey. The rapid movement of their small convoy became a joust between themselves and the ocean which pounded in great sheaves of glistening droplets up along the tortoise

shell. The bell jar they were sitting in was less than perfectly constructed and the wetness creeped in through the seals continuing to spray upon the Princes and her two bunny friends who took to laughter as they found they could do nothing more.

On they sailed, for many multiples of miles, across the Mediterranean Sea cascading like an unruly cork down one trough of the waves and then up to the white crests and then over again the height of which Baron Nelson estimated were four feet high or better.

Once Isabella had put any discomfort she was experiencing to the back of her mind, she took a turn at appreciating the wonderment of looking out to the open sea from her glass enclosure.

The sea waves bended before Isabella as a never ending, undulating table of ultramarine blue, that carved the horizon with it's half curved scythe waves, whose tops were dipped into bowls of sugary, white icing.

Isabella was once again lulled into a blank melancholia, a vacuum with no boundaries and no light at the end of any tunnel. She could easily have remained adrift on a forever voyage of little worth and no purpose, but the entire image disrupted when the mermaids, again in unison, screeched at the turtle that it must make preparations to stop.

Baron Nelson pulled open his spy glass and stood up. As he looked in the direction they were traveling, he explained that a rock formation was rising from up out of the waters. There appeared to be a small opening in the face of the rock, just to the side of a dense grouping of seaweed and this opening grew larger in dimension the closer they came .

"The image I am seeing," commented Baron Nelson, "must be the entrance to the Queens fortress," and then suddenly felt nervous about entering into the stomach of a mountain with no soldiers and no weapons for protection but that of his two hip pistols and sword .

The turtle transport slowed to nothing faster than a puppy dog paddle and the opening in the rock, when taken full on, was in reality far wider and far taller than Baron Nelson had given report.

The threshold to the opening was protected with a camouflage of hanging seaweed which wagged its sinewy, wet arms upon the floating turtle envoy as it floated into the cave.

Within a second of a breath the three visitors found themselves shadowed from the sun light and sailed into the first portion of an immense cavern.

The turtle stopped next to a long slab of smooth granite with a fine covering of moss that acted like a carpet. The formation of thi s dock was leveled to the conformity of the mermaids who used it to slither up onto and where they could primp or sleep the jittery sleep pattern unique to the species of this fan tailed mammal with one eye closed while the other eye was left open in the event that predators may try taking them unawares.

The nasty (and let us be quite honest in calling these two mermaid guides "nasty"); the nasty mermaid guides motioned with their web-hands for Isabella and her friends to move from the turtle and onto the mushy loading dock. Isabella lifted her body carefully from the uncomfortable seat knowing that one of her muscles in her back or her legs might have fallen to sleep and that she could suffer a minor tear inside her limbs if she were not careful.

This slow motion movement also enabled Isabella time to gather her thoughts, wipe the salt water from her face and think about Baron Nelson and his sweetheart Emma, whom Isabella imagined were the two most water laden bunnies in the wide world.

The mermaids wiggled off their seats and submerged into the water up to the level of their clavicle bones as the trio of ambassadors from the Intrepid climbed with unsure legs out onto a flat slippery moss which eventually merged with a stone path going in the direction they concluded would take them to the Queen of the Seal's throne room.

The cave waters surrounded the path which was composed of chiseled rocks in perfect geometric patterns; some with natural coloring that you would expect any sea rock to be, and some giving Lady Emma the presentiment that they were actual gem stones.

The two Nastys' swam several yards before them and waved with their star shaped fins for the visitors to continue following as they communed between themselves with what appeared to be, a cruel laughter mocking of Isabella and her friends.

"I quite wonder if this is the safest place for us to be?" whispered Baron Nelson to Princess Isabella as he secured one paw on a pistol handle and the other on his sword casing. "Perhaps you and Lady Emma should turn about; I shall lie and tell this Queen that the both of you have sea sickness and are too weak to accompany myself. At least you will have a running start if this egotistical fish has set a trap for us."

It was not as if Isabella had not thought of this possibility, and not as if she was unconcerned for her life and that of her Baron, but the greater thought was for that of the safety of Lady Emma and her expectant children.

"We shall be fine my Baron, never fear ; the stars are in our favor," said Princess Isabella Rose whom upon relating this aged old cliche' felt embarrassed for having spoken it. ("All the same," she reasoned, "on behalf of Baron Nelson's concern, I might just as well awake from my dream if there is to be any real threat for my future nieces and nephews.")

The path continued to wind deep into the interior of the mountain where large stalactites hung down giving the appearance of energized lightning bolts. There were lighted, tallow candles held in intricacy molded brass candelabras embedded along the path which emitted a dark smoke that hung in the air at the same level of Baron Nelsons and Lady Emma's heads causing both of them to cough .

"I'm pretending that I am in a fragrant garden," said Princess Isabella sharing with her bunny friends the same difficulty in breathing as a thousand West End London mill workers had done that day.

Isabella also laughed to herself as she slogged along in her soaked battle uniform which was so unusually heavy it was as if she were carrying milk cartons full of mercury in each of her coat and pant pockets.

"And I would like to pretend that my teeth are not chattering," said Baron Nelson as his jaw moved uncontrollably up and down between coughs as he forced the enunciation of words beyond his whiskers .

"I have no idea of what either of you are referring to," stated Lady Emma in a sarcastically, humorous voice.

"And will you be quoting our national proverb of ' chin up' my dear?" asked Baron Nelson in between chatters .

"My chin is 'up', and chattering just as yours, Love." "Tisk," was all the Baron could offer In reply.

On they tramped, following the mermaids whose bodies gleamed with fabulous intensity from the torch light flecks intermixing with the water splashing upon them.

The cave narrowed the further they walked, and this, Baron Nelson surmised acted as a natural defense against potential invaders who instead of rushing towards the Queen of the Seals in hoards, could come only in pairs or triplets, and be cut off by scythes rather neatly. At one point the Nastys' instructed the trio to stop, and as they paused as a great rush of wind came crashing down from a flume carved out of the roof of the cave. The wind blew upon Isabella and her friends and had the effect of drying their clothes to the same degree of having walked an entire day in the Gobi desert.

The tornado of air stunned the three visitors and when it ceased just as suddenly as it had started Isabella found her two friends somehow entwined in around her legs; wrapped bundles of fur all but suffocated in her pant legs.

As Princess Isabella unraveled her Baron and his wife intended, a voice began to wail to them from somewhere down the curvature of the cave and sounded more siren than both of the Nastys' cries together.

"I think we can all agree this is no time to be hesitant," said the tempestuous voice from somewhere down the curvature of the walled corridor.

"Come forward Princess Isabella," commanded The Queen of Seals "and introduce me to your small, furry friends."

Isabella obeying the voice, walked bravely and was followed by Baron Nelson who was whispering to Lady Emma with a huff, "small, furry friends; indeed!"

The three visitors had only to walk one hundred feet or more until they came to the throne room of the Queen which was a large conch shell imbedded in the gut of the cave and giving off the feeling of a place of great serenity and sanctity.

From the shell ceiling hung a most spectacular, circular chandelier lighted with thousands of candles and emphasized with innumerable glass and crystal ornaments, all of which seemed to Isabella had been created for the purpose of directing attention to Her Majesty the Queen who rested loquaciously under it.

The Queen who in Lady Emma's opinion was not particularly attractive, (more like a bloated fish posing as an idyllic theater actress) languished on a long driftwood recliner covered with glistening green seaweed.

The servant mermaids pulled themselves out of the water and sat on smaller portions of driftwood, one at either side of the queen, both of them having picked up poles with jagged coral formations propped on the ends no doubt to be used as miniature harpoons had the queen's life been threatened in any way.

The queen dressed herself in a way that suggested she was due the respect of her inherited position. She wore an ostentatious jewel encrusted crown, a sheer ruby colored robe which was highlighted with ornamental gems; diamonds and sapphires, and she held a golden staff with a petrified starfish on top with its arms sprawled out in five directions on top.

Isabella and her 'furry friends' bowed at the waist without offering a word and waited patiently until the Queen looked them over as if they were of no more importance than fish in the market ready to be wrapped in paper and taken horne to fry.

"Princess Isabella," said the Queen who with the greatest indifference held out her left fin as a sign of greeting.

Isabella held out her left hand and shook the queen's fin with a dainty, impersonal shake. "These M'Lady are Baron Nelson and Lady Emma," said Isabella putting out her arms and bringing both bunnies close to her body.

"So I see you are partial with the beasts of the field; so much so that you will put on a uniform and fight with them; how," and here the Queen allowed her sentence to linger as if she could not conjure the right word to belittle them with .

And then she continued: "How enchanting"; which was a word that could be used in a cuddly, childlike fairy tale, or put in the manor the Queen directed it, was a subtle affront to Princess Isabella and used as 'simplistic', meaning 'inane', 'juvenile', or to the extreme : 'insane'.

Lady Emma was not interested in listening to the joust that was formulating between Isabella and the Queen, but rather focused her imagination upon the Queen's right fin which came to a fine point.

And there, wrapped around her massive front fin on a slight brass bracelet was an enormous pearl ring which was of such a size that Emma's mind conjured a naughty plan (similar to the ones we all have had on occasion and yet never followed through with), about giving the location to the Queen's conch shell and selling it to pirates. "Just wanting to show off her ring; the conceited tart," said Lady Emma to herself.

Isabella responded to the haughty queen whose face, by no exaggeration, was heaped upon with a clay like substance forming a cosmetic mask where the only real part you could see of her face was her two eyes and her thin, rogue colored lips.

This mask made it impossible to 'read' the queen's facial expressions and yet simply listening to the tone in her voice which condescended like a net of intrigue always challenging the listener into a sidestep defense position with the purpose of breaking them into the lowest possible position.

The Queen's posture was also condescending; especially the way she looked down from her throne at her visitors making even someone with the reputation of a famous British naval officer feel as if the troops under his command had just been routed by an inferior navy.

"So, my friend Isabella; if I may call you my friend", continued the Queen "So you have donned a military uniform, shorn your hair that you now have the look of a ship's cabin boy, and have braved the icy waters of my landscape all at the threat of a worthless, yet sad to say, a powerful crustacean."

"Suppose this grand adventure you have chosen for yourself is some elaborate trap of your own conjuring but in reality will whisk you into enslavement where you find yourself enslaved tilling the fields of the earth and fetching water until your days run out?"

With this bit of insult running off the Queen's lips Isabella saw the two mermaids "tee' heeing" behind their hands, pretending to cover their mouths but not disguising the belligerency of their eyes.

"You are indeed kind to think your way through this potential kidnapping exercise Queen Mother; I should feel myself well served by those loyal to you if they have brought you reconnaissance that is contrary to that offered my office."

(The concept itself was indeed absurd for no nation on earth would move against the Crown of England to steal its Princess; no rogue worthy the title indicating him to perform as a " rogue" would have the audacity to even think of such a thing. It was only catty manipulation of the Queen of the Seals who prided herself to be something other than what she was: an old hag.)

Isabella would play the Queen's game but only to a degree and, she would certainly not allow her title denigrated as if it were an old bone cast into the yard for the delight of dogs to gnaw upon .

"Actually, Dear Child," continued Queen , "my spies, friends and double agents tell me that your path is sure, if not fraught with great danger. But I of course cannot let an armada the size of yours pass through my waters without there being a certain degree of respect paid me."

Again the bodyguard mermaids " tee' heed" behind their webbed hands as Isabella looked to Baron Nelson to see if he had come prepared to "pay" respect to their Queen Hag.

"Might I interject here Me' Lady," referring to Princess Isabella while bowing deferentially to the Queen "In the haste of our preparations for battle you may have forgotten your order to me about a gift being in good taste; a thank you to her highness the Queen for her help heretofore as the Indomitable and our other craft travel upon her waters."

Lady Emma coughed suddenly while muttering that she might have taken up a slight chill from the conch shell voyage. In truth Lady Emma had feigned her cough that she might deliver a believable distraction on behalf of her man's emphasis of the word "her".

Unbeknownst to his Princess, Lord Nelson had appropriated something of his own choosing to give as an accessory to the problem box and with his paw retrieved from a small satchel that hanged from his belt loop; a string of pearls with a ruby center piece. Reaching for the satchel became an unintended tense moment as the bodyguard mermaids simultaneously raised their spears and posed themselves able to thrust them flying into the poor bunny's body.

Isabella swung her hands up openly in the "stop" position as Lady Emma coughed out another warning.

Baron Nelson hesitated momentarily but continued retrieving the gift before lifting it to the Queen as "payment" for the rights of passage across her claim of her watery real estate.

"Oh how lovely," said the queen barely glancing at the gemstones while handing the necklace to one of her 'girls' whom had lowered her harpoon weapon and took it for herself placing the stones around her neck and began playing with them as if they were a child's costume jewelry.

Baron Nelson showed no response to this affront and to Isabella his sovereign, though both of them seethed inside knowing that they should soon leave the seal lair lest they wrestle the impudent strumpet to the ground and tear the necklace from the bodyguard; perhaps punching her in the face as well.

"While the necklace was primarily my choosing Your Highness," said Baron Nelson rescuing the moment. I also have this other treasure which Princess Isabella has conceived giving you. From another satchel that hung on the inside of his uniform, Baron Nelson, this time reaching for the problem box, the poised mermaids with their harpoons at the ready watching, produced the small wooden gift and handed it to the Queen's outstretched flipper and he then stepped back from her pedestal.

First the Queen turned the box to look at every side several times and then placed it before her, tapping at what she determined was the opening and watched with delight as it popped open thus displaying the dancing sticks.

"Oh my!" she said with a cheery, childishness in her voice. "Dancing sticks, are they not, Princess Isabella?"

"Yes, Your Highness," said Isabella respectfully and taking a side glance from her Baron and another from Lady Emma, all three being relieved that the gift seemed sufficiently acceptable.

"I shall entertain myself with them later," said the Queen who was actually smiling to the degree that the cake covering her face began to crease at the ends of her lips. The Queen then set the box down neatly and closed the lid. "I am well delighted to have made your acquaintance Princess Isabella," said the Queen of the Seals, and also made reference to Baron Nelson and his betrothed Lady Emma by bowing her head to them as she could not remember their names.

"My whales shall accompany you as far as the Tremular Straights and from that destination we shall wish you great victory and bounties beyond your wildest dreams that you be compensated for all your efforts," said the Queen Hag.

"Then onward Princess Isabella and adorable bunnykins," she said in a bombastic theatrical tone, extending her flippers to the ribs of the conch shell ceiling as if she had power to call down blessings from the god's!"

It was not until Princess Isabella, Baron Nelson and Lady Emma arrived back at the Indomitable once again soaked to the skin, changed into dry clothing and communed in the Captain's quarters did Isabella illiterate her summation of the event.

"Then onward Princess Isabella, and may Zeus and all the god's light your way to victory with searing lightning bolts!" mocked Isabella raising her tea cup up over her head as Baron Nelson's and Lady Emma's cups and saucers which were resting on their laps clattered as they bounced with laughter.

"I say, " stated Baron Nelson once he composed himself and resumed his rigid spine sitting position "those two vixens the old Hag tows along are a frightful bunch."

"I kept counting the seconds wondering when the moisture in the shell would work to dislodge the cement from the Old Girl's face," smirked Lady Emma while she and the others began again to laugh.

After a few more refreshing gibes at the expense of the Queen, Princess Isabella put down her cup and saucer to indicate that the business of the war must now resume .

Lady Emma, understanding this gesture silently excused herself by bowing to Princess Isabella and walked out gingerly shutting the cabin door behind her.

"Well, Baron Nelson ... ," said Isabella directly not completing her sentence as it was Baron Nelson whom was addressed by a midshipman who had knocked for permission to enter the state room.

There was an unpleasant streak of urgency on the face of this petty officer and an excuse of deference to his Princess as he pulled his rabbit commander aside to whisper in his ear.

"Well, M'Lady," said Baron Nelson after the brief dispatch, who was looking at his Princess with the most disconcerting frown, "my midshipman has informed me the King Clam has secured the services of a certain, Black Squid."

"I have not heard of such a one," responded Isabela with a dependent, childlike ring in her voice thus giving her Baron the respect due his troubled demeanor.

"Quite literally Mi' Lady, this Black Squid is a terror to all creatures of the ocean currents. No one knows his exact capabilities but it is said he, or should we say It, was the leading combatant to take down the Spanish Armada enroot to battle Drake and not, as commonly rumored, the winds and the sea.

"He is then, a mercenary; rather, It, is mercenary," equated Isabella out loud having no concern for the creature's gender.

"Yes, Mi' Lady and this is how the KIng Clam secured 'It' for service. The squid is known to

go deep into the caverns of the earth's terrain and remain in his inky, black hovel once It has had It's fill of blood and destruction. It is a beast from another realm; I say "And now it appears the squid is hungry for blood again," said Isabella in a contemplative mood.

A few rolls of the Intrepid against the tides of the sea more and Isabella looked to Baron Nelson stating with complete conviction, "It, our squid monster, is of nothing to us. Full speed ahead my Baron; weather the god's be for us or against us, we shall triumph, and we shall open the sea ways that all may be free to pass!"

Baron Nelson could not contain the prideful smile that contorted his facial muscles causing him to grin, but immediately regained control, rose to his hind feet, bowed to his Princess and left the room without speaking another word.

The waves continued beating upon the hull of the Intrepid paced in rhythm as ticks from the hand of a clock. Isabella could have asked penetrating questions about this sea monster that made its home in inky caverns of the earth's crust, but to what end? She had undertaken this battle for the right of the Righteous; the Little Ones; those who were unable to defend themselves.

To fear the Squid would be to allow its power over herself. No, this day and everyday she purposed to comfort those in need and destroy those who would disrupt peace.

And yet Isabella was neither of the uninformed nor of the very whims of gods whom she had made capricious laughter only minutes before with her friends . If this 'squid of terror' had been set about to destroy the Intrepid and all the other crafts of her navy she reminded herself that even in fairytales there is the potential for bad endings .

Isabella listened to the intense rumble above her head as deck of the Intrepid clutter with the rushing of feet and claws at the command of her Baron to make full flight into battle.

Princess Isabella favored joining the enthusiastic call to arms but knew her place of greatest importance was the floor of her own state room which she met with her knees and enjoined her utterances of humble, silent prayer.

CHAPTER IV

WHAT PRICE VICTORY?

The winds blew in the Intrepids' favor the remainder of the voyage and Baron Nelson watched with great concern and relief that none of the small support crafts had capsized even with the intensity of the jagged seas which jutted up to the sky as if they were mechanical knives in a slaughterhouse.

As the armada carened closer to the perimeters of King Crabs line of defense a projectile lifted up out from an unseen emplacement, leaving behind it a chortle of black smoke which seemed to lumber in the air not knowing its own purpose when it suddenly stopped and dropped making a direct hit on top of Frog-Frigate, a floatile in the shape of a lily pad.

This medium sized, green colored craft was commandeered by Reginald Toad and housed thirty or more seasoned swamp fighters who propelled the frigate with long-stemmed oars or, in the case of the older sea frogs who thought paddles were for 'the less than seasoned children shipmates' reached forth their long arms and pushed the waters with their large, firm webs.

The frog ship was named after a retired commander, Damien Toad -the craft name being The Damien, splintered like a child's crib made of matchsticks. Fortunately, all crew members escaped unhurt by the metal projectile implanting itself into The Damien and, were able to swim to the safety of one of the other boats that circled the decimated craft.

"And now it begins!" shouted Baron Nelson to those who stood with him on the bridge not the least notable Princess Isabella whom had donned her flack- jacket, a steel bowl like helmet and a gun belt where pistols holstered on either side of her hips hung.

The first mate, kept a telescope glued to his eye and reported the maneuverings of King Clams approaching attack flotillas, and also his stationary troops which were poised on buoys in the water.

There were also screecher spy birds who were seconded to deliver bundles of explosives on to their targets but whom would prove to be horrible shots due to the fact of their light weight and, that King Clam had commanded them to carry far too much munitions to make any negative effect against his enemy Princess Isabella.

The killer whales took position on the left flank and moved in two separate pods of five each. They first appeared on the surface of the water to parade their sinister prowess then dove in unison disappearing like depth charges.

Renegade bottlenose dolphins carened straight on towards all of the small vessels with the intention of capsizing them. There was even a band of dusty old pirates whom themselves and the ship they appeared in had sailed out of an earlier century and looked more like a band of mascots than any real threat.

And with all this the King Clam's subordinates sent up explosive depth charges targeted at the underside of Isabella's crafts. Up they popped like marshmallows in a bowl of hot cocoa but unfortunately for the King Clam, one of his minions had painted over their individual valve covers with a red 'letter 'X' for reasons even a clam could not explain.

So easy was the 'X' to see in the water that Isabella's sailors had time to check their horse racing schedules before maneuvering around them or blasting them for target practice with shots from their shouldered rifles.

Another trick the mad Clam used was to send seagulls over the armada to drop sprinkle bomb pellets onto the deck of every ship. The Clam King took great pride in these deadly pellets having invented them himself.

Inside each pellet delivered was a nest of termites. Once the termites hit the deck of the wooden ships they would burrow themselves into the structure and begin their work by gnawing away until the boat collapsed and sunk. The only difficulty with this scheme was that it takes termites years to eat their way through wood and by that time not only would the battle be over but the rest of this book as well. (Sorry Mr. Clam King, you looser !)

There were other invented means of attacking Isabella's Armada; there were large harpoons situated on flat rafts and powered by tenacious turtles who guided these rafts into the sides of Isabella's ships and the evil sailors would jump off at the last possible second before the harpoons hit their target.

Again they were wonderfully unsuccessful as the rafts weight was displaced once the turtles left the craft which caused the raft to bounce and, then roll over and sink just split seconds before impact. And the only one harpoon that touched anything of concern was the one that hit a double fortified tin container owned by the Sardinian Sardine family and lent out to Horatio Grasshopper, a valiant gent who had the great distinction among the grasshopper genus to be able to read Farsi, a language from the land of Iran where he picked it up while in his early years flying rear bomber-directional guide with a swarm of locust.

Horatio was quite proud of himself having learned the language so readily, relying heavily upon the accomplishment and feeling himself a bit superior to any of his colleagues, Horatio often dropped in a word or two during tea time, and then excused himself while stupidly saying "Oh, there goes my Farsi again; just can't seem to get beyond it."

But he was a good seaman to have on the team, rather, a good sea-grasshopper. And when that harpoon hit his double enforced sardine can Horatio simple cropped open his wings and flapped above the carnage.

There were other forms of maneuvering and types of destruction Princess Isabella and Lord Nelson observed from the bridge of the Intrepid. A clever series of floating buoys disguised as rock formations ejected endless streams of thick smoke.

The smoke was so dense that it confused the landscape and made it difficult for Isabella's armada to navigate through the waters. It also made the attacks upon Isabella's convoy difficult for King Clam's. The Clam's firing missiles which came from every direction in no particular order sunk more of their own vessels than that of Isabella's.

One particularly large explosive sent from King Clam's private fortress careened off course and hit directly upon the two killer whale pods. The pods were engulfed with an enormous plume of water splashing all ten mammals were cast higher than a ship mast. And then, another force of water met them when they came tumbling down acting like one big hand which lifted them again and beached them all on dry land.

So the battle raged that entire day; ships, birds, and fish careened in and out of each other's path, bunnies, mammals and insects wiped their brows with a sooty wetness that when it hit the deck of the ship looked like droplets of mud. Mercifully casualties were few, destruction of property was immense. And then, for no observable reason, the noise and fury of cannon fire ceased and a great white flag went up at King's fortress.

It was not until the last cannon projectile fell -this being another of the crab's artillery efforts (of course badly missing its mark again and this time destroying a laundry rock which was a rock where animals lay open what few clothing pieces they have to dry or air out) when a sudden, curious silence shrouded the landscape.

Isabella's naval troops poised mid movement. The birds screeching overhead shut their beaks with their only sound being that of wind passing along their feather tips.

A series of instruction were given to Baron Nelson's second-in-command and then shouted with the greatest of enthusiasm that a launch was to be lowered and that Baron Nelson and their victorious Princess would be going to encounter King Crab face to shell.

Baron Nelson accompanied by Isabella and a formation of troops left the Intrepid in short order and sailed to the dock leading to King Crab's fortress castle.

Once the launch-ship nestled up to the enemy dock a mass of soldiers in shredded uniforms and deflated egos tied Princess Isabella's craft up to the wood piling and moved away from the lowered gangplank allowing she and her armed entourage to step ashore.

There was a small pathway which led to the King Crab's courtroom which was strewn with broken pieces of building, furniture, and a particularly mangled horse whose four legs had been blown off the central body but had somehow stayed near enough together that it looked as if a blacksmith had removed them for a more convenient way of working on the hooves.

Once inside the King Crab' s private receiving room Baron Nelson could not but comment on the obvious look and feel it had in relation to the interior of Isabella's court and Isabella in return directed his more careful attention to the ceiling which was supported by a crisscross of wooden beams much the same as the natural configuration of the bramble bush in the Court of Forty.

King Crab sat at the end of the room on a slab of granite with an angry scowl painted across his large, flat, half-shell face. A faded, greenish bit of goop dripped in a continuous stream down his left nostril and wend down onto his shoulder and then around his back. His body looked something like a deflated atmospheric balloon stuffed into a pair of miss fitting trousers and a vest which doubled for a dinner bib, having innumerable splotches of food stuffs adhered to it.

As Isabella and Baron Nelson approached the deposed crab a silent wretch of disdain mingled his own discontent through small air inlets on either side of his nose.

"Your Highness," said Baron Nelson to King Crab once Isabella and he had walked the length of the throne room and stood before the large sectional King Crab rested upon. Isabella had to admit to herself that King Crab's large arm extension of eight arms all ending in powerful claws were frightfully intimidating.

Baron Nelson, whom once again was proudly able to demonstrate to his Princess his worth, repeated information garnered from his network of carefully placed spies that King Crab, more than anything else, feared being placed in a boiling pot of water and was hardly a One to risk his soldiers reprisal had he raised one pincer to harm the victorious princess.

"May I introduce to you Your Highness, Princess Isabella," continued Baron Nelson addressing his foe with respect as is proper In the aftermath of a battle.

"Your Highness," said Isabella introducing herself with a curtsey complemented King Crab of his and his soldier's bravery while simultaneously making sincere inquiry about the Crab's wounded warriors.

King Crab used an interpreter to communicate with his conquers though Baron Nelson knew the crab could easily understand the King's English. He responded to Isabella's question that his wounded were being removed from the landscape upon which they had fallen and moved to a well managed animal and fish hospital on the island of Corsica.

A treaty was briefly spoken of with the agreement that the line details would be looked into later by secretaries from both camps. In effect the treaty stated that King Crab would give up his ambitions to control the waterways and live like all of God's creatures in the pursuit of a harmonious life.

King Crab's interpreter asked Princess Isabella and Baron Nelson if they would be interested in staying for lunch. King Crab of course did not care at all about his conquers comfort but, wanting to show he could rise above the level of any ordinary crustacean by showing his military grace in the face of defeat.

And just then as Isabella lifted her voice to respond to the interpreter with the decision to decline the insincere offer, every being in King Clam's throne room, turned his or her attention to a great rush of water that burst through the throne room entrance way.

In a moment Isabella, Baron Nelson, King Crab, every soldier, and every inanimate object was lifted up by these water tides to the height of the vaulted ceiling. The throne room filled so rapidly, that Isabella had no time to do or say anything but to gulp for air.

Isabella began to tumble and turn within the water tide and found she was being sucked as it were out the throne room and back down the entrance path. She lost sight of her Baron and everything solid or tangible and was rumbling and churning in the waves so fast that the entire experience became one of mass of terror.

It seemed to Isabella that she had been washed many miles, and perhaps many days from her war experience in the Mediterranean when she came to the conclusion that she was now lying flat on her back in one of Toad's garden rows looking upwards towards England's evening sky.

CHAPTER III: The Death of Toad, The introduction

of Dinah, and the first appearance of:

The Insidious Mr. Rancid

And so we find, as our story continues, that our heroine Princess Isabella Rose, whom for many years believed her parents that when they told her she was a real princess, found out quite to the contrary that she was nothing more than a little girl.

All the same, Isabella was committed to living in a world of fantasy and had conjured up for herself imaginary friends such as bugs and birds who amazingly spoke to her in comprehendable english.

Notwithstanding, life was soon to change for our young Isabella and, as some stories progress, change does not necessarily work to a favorable end.

Isabella lifted herself from the ground that had once been Toad's neatly manicured garden but was now overrun with water. She then took a few moments of investigation before she found the water hose nozzle was pouring out water.

She followed the hose back to the spigot which had been turned fully open. Isabella turned the spigot counter clockwise until no more water escaped. "What person had perpetrated such a prank upon my adventures in my court?" questioned Isabella angrily and vowed some sort of vengeance upon that person.

As Isabella began to make her way into the manor her conscious thoughts turned immediately to her personal state of affairs which she reasoned could only be remedied with a long, hot bubble bath.

Isabella made her way back to the double glass doors wondering if Edna or Toad would care to bring her a towel so that she might not soil the carpet with her muddy feet. Isabella put her head inside the door and shouted out "Mother! Father!, I need your help."

At first she wondered if she had not yelled loudly enough (after all she told herself haughtily, they were really a couple of very old bats the both of them and surely losing their hearing) and so she called out again but still there was no response from either parent.

After waiting for a few more clicks of the clock Isabella chose to wander in with all of her mud trappings and go into the library to ascend her secret staircase.

The warmth of the tub water came with such calm relief in comparison to the freezing hose water and caused Isabella to let out a great moan as she sunk deep into the froth of the purple colored bubbles.

So much mud flowed out of Isabella's hair and off her skin that after at least one full hour of soaking she reached for a towel and wrapped herself while simultaneously tapping down vigorously with her foot upon the tub drain before it began to swallow the entire residue.

Once her skin was dried she wrapped her head in the towel and went to the dresser and pulled out a fresh nightgown. Isabella then hopped onto her bed, her back once again stiff upright against the backboard and breathed deeply. It was only then that Isabella gave thought about the battle, the conquest of King Crab, the Queen Seal; the bumpy ocean ride, being splashed in the face with freezing cold salt water and the wonderful faces and voices of her friends Baron Nelson and Lady Emma.

A flood of tears shot out upon Isabella's face and rolled down to her chin as she had sometime done when she had slurped her soup and a sharp reprimand came from her mother. What could have happened? Had her two friends drowned; or were they so frightened of the flood waters that they realized they could no longer play their parts in Princess Isabella's fairytale?

Having exhausted herself with worry, and weeping great ripples of sorrow, Isabella fell into a deep, restless several hour sleep with the faces of crabs, mermaids and bunnies vying for her attention, talking to her and even shouting at her!

It was still day when Isabella woke with a start and found herself immensely refreshed as if all of her life to that moment and including her adventures with the Court of Forty had been nothing but a dream from which she had personally grown in strength and wisdom. Isabella could find no explanation for this feeling but that she had been as it were a character in a serial novel and now had closed the book upon its last chapter and was ready to begin her next adventure.

Isabella touched the top of her head finding her hair bone dry, and to the point of causing her to laugh out loud, she noticed that with the wrestling with the characters of her imagination she had kicked off both of her socks and saw one of them was hanging from her metal bed post and the other an arm toss across the floor the same as been read to her of some other fairy tale character.

Isabella stretched and yawned and bound off her bed and, leaving her room with the purpose of commanding her parents to feed her.

As Isabella descended the stairs to the lower floor she found it odd that she was unable to hear Toad's radio playing and went with an uneasy sense of curiosity into his den to see if perhaps the radio had been removed and taken up into his tiny repair shop in the attic. But the radio was there and Isabella placed her hand to the control button where symphonic notes of Bach filtered out of the speakers like grains of sand caught on a drift of air.

Satisfied with her answer to the question about the workability of the radio (but not with the unanswered question of why Toad had neglected to keep it playing), Isabella began to walk to the other rooms of the manor calling out timidly, "Mother, Toad," calls that were answered with a death silence.

Isabella walked into the kitchen, the dining room, opened the door to the pantry, the closets and even went into Toad's library to put her hand on the secret door panel which opened to the basement but decided not to press it as she reasoned that Toad would never have taken Edna to his secret labyrinth and was surely not there then. And with this understanding Isabella realized for the first time in her life she was helplessly alone. Isabella was alone; and when she was certain she was alone, Isabella stepped rapidly up the stairs hastily closing the door to her bedroom.

It is enough to say that Isabella had never experienced isolation. There was always Edna, Toad, or books, or her animal and insect friends to keep her company and to comfort her. And now for the first time since her days in infancy Isabella had to rely upon herself to tell herself who she was altogether and not allow circumstances to do it for her.

Isabella reacted to this realization by hastily propping a chair against the bedroom door. She wedged the back of the chair into the door handle so the handle would not turn.

Isabella then took the Captain of the artillery guard, Sir Charles, a toy soldier who was standing stiffly awaiting his next orders, a very young man who had proved himself valiant in battle and like she, escaped the flood. She ordered Sir Charles to stand on the top back of the chair and to shoot intruders, but not kill them .

A peculiar thought entered Isabella's mind right at this time and she asked herself the question of "What would Alice do?" (This of course is our friend Alice who found herself in the mysterious Wonderland and who ventured there with all her beauty, wit, and a certain cat named Dinah.)

A cat! Isabella concluded; she was in need of a cat. After all she reasoned, Alice was a girl someone had taken all the effort to write a book about. She was someone of great worth; if not 'charisma', which is another thing Alice took with her when she leapt down the rabbit hole. The word 'charisma' is a word Toad had taught his daughter.

"You can remember the word Isabella," said Toad in his school master voice, "by linking three small words together: "charm" -"is" -"ME" or translating the word "me" into the French vocabulary it sounds like this: "moui."

And even though Isabella had promised for herself to become the fullness of the word charming, and simultaneously have her parents buy a cat for her to befriend and to tell secrets to, Isabella was still very much alone.

And again as Isabella allowed herself to drift along another path of new things to experience, her keen sense of hearing picked out the slow turning of the front door knob and the unmistakable squeaking of the hinges which moaned like a musical squeeze box while the door opened.

Isabella removed the Captain of the Guard from his post and dislodged the chair while quietly opening the door to her bedroom listening more intently to the slow shuffling of feet which tapped out a familiar sound on the downstairs portico.

"Mother!" cried Isabella with great relief as she left her room moving rapidly down the stair well.

"Where have you been Mother?" asked Isabella as she embraced her mother tightly once she landed on the entrance hall tile.

"Why are you so quiet mother?" asked Isabella not having a return greeting and feeling her mother's body limp and a bit wobbly.

Without saying a word or removing her coat, Edna took Isabella into the sitting room where they lit down together as Isabella waited patiently for her mother to speak.

The moments of silence rolled on and Isabella began to think that the two of them touching was similar to bookends pinched together with no books between them.

Eventually Edna did conjure a very deep breath and began to enunciate something as her voice quivered indicating to Isabella that she was about to hear something unpleasant.

"Is Toad right, Mother?" asked Isabella in a low voice. (Not that she cared much for the fate of Toad but with a desire to show respect for what she could only surmise would be the cause of Edna's grief.)

"No my Dear, Toad is no longer with us," said her mother as she reached for a handkerchief stuffed into her coat arm and placed it up to her eye ducts.

"I am sorry Mother," said Isabella. "I know you loved him."

"I find it curious my child; when Toad was here I was tired continuously of his presence, and now ... ," whimpered Edna reservedly not wanting to upset her daughter simultaneously removing her coat and adjusting the arms of her sweater "I miss him terribly, and it is only a few hours since he was pronounced..."

Edna's words slipped into silence. Isabella felt a touch of grief for her mother and began petting her arm and hand much the way she visualized herself petting a new kitten.

Edna related that Toad had succumbed to a massive heart attack while watering in his garden and that she had called out many times for Isabella before she climbed into the ambulance with her husband and gone off to the hospital.

"There was no need to worry; I was fine," remarked Isabella as she petted her mother's sweater imagining that it might 'meow' had she been able to continue petting until tea.

Isabella and her mother sat silently upon the sofa as the afternoon sun played an entertaining dance for them upon the sitting room furniture.

It first danced a brash display from the bay window where it stealthily crossed the floor, hopping from one throw rug to another and, then climbing onto a portable mahogany server where it heaved up and clashed down hard upon the silver tureen with its burnished surface polish making it almost impossible to look at without hurting your eyes.

And after Isabella thought she and her mother had taken long enough to be reverent for Toad's death, Isabella related to Edna that she no longer felt comfortable crawling around in the bramble and, now that Toad was gone she felt no special interest in tending to the garden whatsoever.

"Mother," said Isabella with no particular introduction to her forthcoming statement "I think we shall get along very well owning a cat."

"A cat?" repeated Edna wondering how in so small a portion of one afternoon Isabella had concluded that she would no longer wished to play in her fortress and also see herself as a responsible owner of a kitten.

But it was set in Isabella's heart and the following day Edna found herself taking the cab to the nearest animal shelter with precise instructions for the perfect animal to fulfill Isabella's orders.

"You fluffy, white ball!" exclaimed Isabella as her mother took the kitten from the carrying box and place it in Isabella's arms. "She feels so much like a hand-muff mother! Yes, she is so perfect!"

As Isabella nestled her little friend she announced "Oh Dinah, you are just what I have always wanted!"

It would not be longer than one or two meals that the new resident of the Pulstar Manor felt herself comfortable wearing a bib around her neck sitting in a child's high chair and joining the family gathering for supper.

Isabella used an even swing of motion as she brought the kittens food from her very own china plate and placed the fork daintily up to Dinah's lips and with equal ease interchanged a baby's bottle filled with milk.

"She's so adorable," Edna would say of Dinah who sat at the head of the table where Toad had once taken his seat. This decision, Isabella reasoned, of her mother insisting that Dinah sit where once her husband had, was an unconscious motivation to exchange a balding, stern face with one that had the all the delights of childhood curiosity backed by the innocence of a non-Edwardian personality.

It was not many weeks into the wake of Toad's passing, his small, practically unattended funeral; the unpleasant task of going through his personal belongings and either giving them to the shelter or simply sealing them in boxes and then stacking them into one of the corners of his library, that Edna, Isabella, and Dinah found they were getting along quite nicely, thank you; thank you very much!

After lunch one day Isabella excused herself and began clearing dishes. "Oh, don't bother Dear," her mother said in a glowing voice as if by some happenstance of miracles, she was in her early years of marriage again, with not one but two children to care for "why don't you take Dinah outside and take in the sunshine before the fog rolls back?"

"But I do want to help with the dishes Mother."

"I am quite competent my dear; I can assure you. I was giving large dinner parties for Toad and his business associates long before you came to visit us for the first time."

And this is how Edna always spoke about Isabella's sudden appearance on the Pulstar Manor steps: "The first time Isabella had corne to visit". It was as if Isabella's arrival by mysterious, and yes, obviously, wrong means was something equal to a person of goodwill dropping off a packet of clothing to the Salvation Army.

"Mother," persisted Isabella "do you ever think we shall be hiring the services of a maid?" Edna put her fork down on the china plate with a clank as her face went suddenly ashen. "A maid?" uttered Edna as if Isabella had suggested they invite into their kitchen a jackal.

"We shall not be in need of a maid, my dear," said Edna as she swallowed the remaining parcel of mutton in her mouth and washed it with a big swallow of port.

"It's just that someday I shall be going off to school like all of the other children and perhaps you shall need help cleaning? The maid might become a close friend of yours as well. Rosalind and Charles have a maid and her name is Miss Pringle. She often gives them advice on things such as her favorite pick in the horse races."

"Rosalind and Charles!" exclaimed Edna as if she had not heard Isabella correctly.

"Yes, they are on the wire when you take your nap in the afternoon mother. Their show is called 'The Jaunty Adventures of Rosalind and Charles' . Dinah and I listen to them every day. Miss Pringles has a funny laugh; something like a horse neighing. Dinah always lifts her head from my lap when Miss. Pringles laughs. I quite expect her to be asking for a bag of oats and barley."

"This is nonsense Isabella; I must say. Now do as I have suggested and take your kitten into the garden; look the sun is threatening to move behind the clouds. You had better hurry!"

And so Isabell a unknotted the bib form Dinah's neck and picked her up in her arms "Come Miss Dinah the world of adventure awaits us," said Isabella and carried her kitten out the double doors and into the fresh air not at all suspecting the real adventures that lay before them.

Chapter III (Part Two)

Edna did not finish with the last few bites of vegetables but, instead stared at the felt covered wallpaper with its intricate designs by William Morris as if she were looking into the twisted arms of a wall of ivy which had been shorn of all its leaves .

If anyone had been living in a fantasy world it was Edna and not her daughter Isabella. The prophetic verse from the book of Ecclesiastes that 'time and chance happens to all of God's creatures' would mean nothing less than Isabella leaving to go into a school for orphaned children while she, Edna, would live her final days in a prison nursing home as some insipid Candy Striper serving her medication hee -hawed like a donkey.

"What is to become of us Oh, Lord?" asked poor Edna as tears began to well in the poor widow's eyes.

In neither Toad's nor Edna's lives there had been little use for God or things of the spiritual realm. Instead they faced all of life's difficulties with the British adverb of "keeping your chin up."

But these last few weeks with Toad's passing, had given Edna much time to conclude for herself that life around the Manor would someday soon have to change and that answers beyond her capability would, as the Rector of St . Michael's said, "be in the hands of God".

No matter how many times Edna nestled her face into the Dinah's soft fur or sat with her afternoon tea telling Isabella about her time growing up, the names of her dolls, the summer holidays she and her family took every year to Cambridge visiting Auntie, and Grandpa Pa, there would come a day when truth would have to be met directly on.

And as 'time and chance' always travel their own schedules, Edna did not have to wait to take her last drink from her crystal goblet when the doorbell rang out.

"My," said Edna with her lips parted but not certain if she had really spoken the word or simply thought it. The bell rang again and as it did, Edna took her serviette up from her lap and pushed her chair from the table taking quick note that the flat tortured ivy vines had formed themselves back to the curly bright patterns of Mr. Morris' own invention.

Had the hooded, spiritless creature with the scythe been the one to have rung the Pulstar Manor bell he would have been a more welcomed sight than the man who stood before Edna as she peered through the door spy glass.

His name was Rancid a character, who had been baptized with a first, middle or perhaps two middle names, and perchance he was Somebody, Something with several numerals behind his surname but Edna knew him only as Rancid and he insisted this is how everyone should address him.

His manner, demeanor, his person as a person could only be described as "creepy"; 'Creepy', a word originating in the English language giving definition to an ill, troubling feeling causative in the human psyche by a mere shake of hands or a gaze such as a black cat treading across your path.

Rancid dressed the dress of an English gentleman to be sure, and spoke with the delicate grace and facility of one born into gentry. He presented an air of being fully accessible by being current with the current-day's 'small talk' .

Due to his position and wealth he floated at the highest levels of society and never failed to make use of this position to further his one passion: Power.

For this accumulation, Mr. Rancid, carried an accumulative file of deceptive weaponry keeping them at the ready much the same as professional magician keeps an assortment of playing cards neatly tucked in his vest.

Rancid set himself apart from the other "gentlemen" at the British swares' and brokered deep liaisons in the saber tooth tiger cages of female gossip.

Rancid was always one to entertain a potential barter; one bit of knowledge about whom might be sleeping with whom in return for a few minutes with one of the ladies husbands who might be abreast of a business opportunity for him to fulfill.

Oh how fun this was for our Mr. Rancid, quite the unheralded toast of any gathering; to sit next to him in the side parlor always enhanced ones position of a person being in "the know" not so sure if your best friend was about to be socially assassinated or you, yourself. Inroads to the silly conversations and gossip of women who were all too busy protecting their reputations fending off against their female competitors was a simple and delicious to Mr. Rancid as Yorkshire Pudding.

"Good afternoon Edna," said Rancid tipping his hat, as a sickening waft of cigar smoke engulfed her breathing area. "I do hope I am not disturbing you in your time of morning."

It was tempting of course for Edna to conjure up the memory of when the muscles in her arms were strong, when in girls prep school she was the champion archer for both her junior and senior years and where she could now use that strength to slam the door in Rancid's face; but alas the spirit was willing and the flesh was so very tired. "I have just finished tea Mr. Rancid do come in and allow me to take your hat and cape."

Rancid entered the Pulsar Manner as if he were an honored Statesman sent as an ambassador on an intrepid mission. "Please," said Edna motioning with her hand that Rancid might step into the drawing room. "May I offer you tea, Sir," asked Edna surprised at her demeanor which could not have been placed in more of a topsy-turvy challenge than if she were on the roll-a-coaster at The Piccadilly carnival.

"I thank you, no, I shant' be having tea," said Rancid as he sat in the chair offered him. Edna sat in the opposite high back, her body rigid; her fingers entwined tightly resting upon her lap awaiting what tepid deception Rancid would spew out first.

"I must say Edna, I am sorry to have missed your husband's funeral. He was such an honorable man; so fastidious in all of his endeavors. He truly will be missed in the community."

Edna responded by saying "He was an honorable man as you have said; loyal and forthright." Edna, in any other person's company would, with a brief sentence more, include in her response that Toad's life was much enhanced by those of his profession and personal life as well. But in Rancid's case nothing could be further from the truth and Edna did not want to add any more to the charade than was already being staged under her roof.

Edna made a quick, subconscious look around her shoulder. Perhaps another prayer to her Lord would have been the most expedient, most assured way to tell her daughter "please, by no means come into this house while this 'creature' sits here!"

Rancid not quite sure about Edna's action, cleared his voice as Edna turned her head quickly around. "Are you certain this is an appropriate time to visit?" inquired Rancid in his most diplomatic tone of voice.

"I know that you have come on business Mr. Rancid. You may proceed with it."

Rancid reached into a small valise he had packed under his arm and pulled a singular file opening it across his lap. Rancid lifted his spectacles from the interior of his vest taking an annoying amount of time to wipe them off.

"The matter is simple, Mrs. Tumblers, your husband Mr. Tumblers, with his passing, has released all dictatorial powers on the board of trustees and we shall be putting out the vote posthaste for his replacement. We of course need only your signature that all private notations from his files are made public to the board; he, as you know, was a copious record keeper and they most certainly are all up-to-date . We have need of your signature only Mrs. Tumbler's , and, of course, the combination to his small office safe."

For all of the many years Edna had pleaded with her husband that he share the business of the bank and in the case of his association with Rancid and the affairs of the Children's Receiving Home, Edna confessed to herself that in her way of pouting and getting even with him while even refusing him conjugal rights she had never put up enough protestation where he would relent. Toad never thought it 'proper or professional' as he stated it, to divulge even the slightest of details. "

And if he were to relate anything at all about his affairs on the Receiving Home board it would be when he was hanging up his coat in the hall closet and putting his dainty feet into his dainty maroon colored slippers and say "all went well today, thank you".

Edna knew about her husband's office safe having visited him there each Friday before the birth of Amaranth when he would take her to lunch. And though she had no knowledge of what her husband kept locked away Edna believed there was nothing of any worth in the safe to be concerned with. Everything Toad kept of value he kept at the Manor in the library; his gem collection in the basement and this of course included the stone.

Thus with an impish smile Edna answered the portly Rancid by saying she had no knowledge of the combination for the safe or any place her late husband may have kept a paper with the numbers written on it.

Just the same, Edna felt it dutiful to allow Rancid complete access to the day-to-days of Toad's banking notations which he kept neatly filed in the library. "And," she maintained "I would not be surprised if my husband kept an encyclopedia of notations from the very day he began his banking career; I must say I do not envy you or your secretary when you mill through them. (Indeed, Mrs. Tumbler's had, in the cleaning out of Mr. Tumbler's personal remains, found to her incredulous disbelief -stashed behind Toad's sock drawer, in, as it were a 'secret compartment', a small wooden box containing strands of hair that he had obviously pulled from his brush and placed neatly side to side).

"My responsibility, Sir," continued Edna having lifted her chin with pride "was to provide Mr. Tumblers a safe haven from the wiles of the evil world," said Edna breathing in through her nostrils as if she were a lioness on the savannah sniffing out potential harm for her cubs in the tall grasses.

"I see," said Rancid in a tone that would indicate he was not thoroughly convinced. Rancid put his head down as if his soul were entangled in consternations when in reality he was thinking about having a pint at the tavern.

With a slow gesture he clasped together the file on his lap, removed his spectacles from his face and before putting them back in his vest held them out to Mrs. Tumblers as any accomplished esquire might before making a directive to a court.

"There might, my Dear Mrs. Tumblers, be one other avenue of approach," but just then, before -as Edna assumed- Rancid would disseminate an invective of threat, there was the turning of the knob of the double glass doors and the entering of Isabella and her kitten .

"Who is with you mother?" asked Isabella hearing the gravel voice of Rancid and smelling the dull fragrance of cigar smoke that came from his clothing and permeated the room .

"My dear!" said Edna all but hitting the ceiling lamp when she jumped out of her chair as if a depth charge had exploded under her seat.

Edna whisked her weight of being and fluffed her skirt around Isabella as a mother duck does when directing she perceives her ducklings of being endangered.

"You should go outside dear; we are engaged in a business meeting," said Edna with great strain in her voice.

"And who is this delightful chap?" asked Rancid who himself had bounded from his seat as well , a man who never underestimated a stressful situation which so often carried along with it the potential to leveraging a weight upon some other person's weakness .

"This is my..." began Edna whose imagination for explaining the presence of her once orphaned child gave her the facial expression of a wax museum figure.

"You're which . .?" said Rancid whose mind was racing with so much conspiratorial curiosity he could not keep his Cheshire cat smile from showing.

"I am Anubis," proclaimed Isabella.

"Anubis!" hummed Rancid in a deleterious voice. "Not The Anibis; Heavens! I seem to recall you were the-talk-of-the-town in Egypt about two thousand BC? My, you have traveled far to be with us this day."

 "She, I mean, he, is Mr. Tumbler's nephew from Kent," said Edna trying to regain her balance as if she were an acrobat surviving a near fatal fall.

"A nephew. .," stated Rancid, "from Kent you say? .. Indeed; a nephew named Anubis from Kent. Has a certain ring of mystery about it; wouldn't you say Lady Tumbler's? I was unaware that your late husband had relations in Kent or anywhere else for that matter. I recall your beloved Toad telling me he was raised an only child. But it would appear I am mistaken; the years seem to be creeping up on me faster than I thought. My, how age does play tricks with one's memory."

"Dear, please shake hands with Mr. Rancid," said Edna hesitantly. Isabella put forth her hand as if she had been instructed to place it into a snake hole.

"Charmed to meet you lad," said Rancid taking Isabella by the hand while Edna recoiled in fear that the old bugger might transmit a communicable disease to her daughter.

"I must say lad this is quite an imaginative name you have come up with for yourself; or is this something of a passing fad among the youth?" said Rancid still holding Isabella's hand and crooking his head while looking at her with a nasty gesture.

"I think dear, you and Dinah should be going back to play in the garden," said Edna taking both Rancid and her daughter's hands and separating them. Dinah who had walked in with Isabella was clawing upon Isabella's leg wanting to be picked up.

"Oh, Dinah," said Isabella taking her kitten into her arms.

"And what a nice hat you would make somebody," gestured Rancid tapping Dinah sharply on the head. Dinah responded to this introduction by taking a violent swipe at Rancid with her outstretched claws and hissing angrily.

"Come now," said Edna who opened the glass doors and herded her daughter out to the garden "we will be only a few minutes more, dear."

Rancid was already back in his chair looking again into his file when Edna closed the doors and returned into the parlor. "I seem to have forgotten this one more item Lady Tumbler's," said Rancid who looked as if he were digging in for a good long discussion.

"Actually Sir," pleaded Edna I did not want to be impolite but there were several things I was about when you rang and I would ask you if we might look into your final point at some other time; say early next week."

"But of course, " said Rancid in the most gentlemanly tone which even on the bare surface sounded like a farcical gesture from a wart covered ogre .

In a few moments Rancid had put away his file and placing it up under his arm and walked to the door. "Here , allow me ," said Rancid as he reached for his coat and top hat and took his very time putting them on his body. "Now Lady Tumblers," he said making a slight bow and opening the door to make as if he were leaving. Instead, Rancid turned to face Edna with a menacing look so pointed it was as if he were regurgitating a vile of ammonia he had just gargled with.

"I am sorry to have come by with nary a moment notice Mrs. Tumblers; yet I think I have not made it clear as to the urgency of my need for the combination to your late husband's safe; if you can just dig in your memory a bit further."

"Just exactly what do you expect to find in the safe Mr. Rancid? Surely there was nothing my husband was hiding that could have been of much concern to you or any other persons on the board . The only thing that might be of urgency is that one of his pork sandwiches is molding and is beginning to stink."

Rancid's face contorted in vile disdain but captured itself from teetering over the edge into overt anger. And while adjusting the lay of his cloak Rancid fidgeted with the drawstring and said in closing, "Well, I must be off; early next week then," and with this he turned on his heels and slithered down the path.

(PART III)

Rancid's taxi drove him out through the Tumbrels Down district and to the neighboring iron district, an area unto itself laid upon with industrial grime shot out from factory chimneys and hovered in the air seeping down upon the landscape like an oily blanket falling upon a choleric infant in its crib.

When once at the chosen destination Rancid paid the driver and, for no particular reason cracked hard upon the rump of the horse nearest him with his walking cane.

There was the damnable incline to the Trader's Trove Pub with its crumbling wood stairs that made it potentially treacherous for a creature like Rancid who had suffered from his permanently disjointed left knee.

The knee injury was a life remembrance when in his effort to prove to his thieving friends his worth as he volunteered for the job of jumping from a three story rooftop across to an apartment building window. Once he had climbed through the window Rancid would be in a position to unlatch the inside door to a private apartment and he and his friends would pilfer the belongings.

Rancid jumped barely catching the window ledge with his hands. Unable to swing his feet up his strength gave out and Rancid dropped the three stories to the unforgiving pavement. Rancid remembered his friends who instead of rushing to help him leaned over the building roof jeering and laughing at him while he writhed in pain with a compound fracture to the leg.

Shortly thereafter a crowd gathered around Rancid and when the police arrived they surmised he had been victim of his own misfortune.

93

Rancid fainted many times while being carted to the police station for booking. And though his leg bone jutted from his pant leg, and his blood was making puddles upon the paddy wagon floor, the police took the an indirect route to the station to buy a bag of crumpets first.

Before passing out completely when given the antistatic in the sickbay of the county hospital Rancid remembered the 'pals' who had been with him on the failed robbery and, whom he vowed that each one in their life time would know the same experience of humiliation and suffering.

Rancid noticed that Trader's Trove was all but empty considering it was usually full with the first wave of derelicts walking from the factories and hanging about for "one more pint before they went home to beat their wives and children.

"Game's on Mr. Rancid, said the obese bartender Mr. Chaseman, who was wearing the tattered, never-clean apron he used to both wipe out glasses and pick his nose. "None of the lads want to miss the finals.

"Ye' ot' to be putting a wire in ' ere Mr. Chaseman; wouldn't be loose'en as much business, Sir" said Rancid taking his pint.

Now if you have noticed Mr. Rancid's way of speaking has taken on a new identity. Oh how clever Mr. Rancid is; more like a chameleon lizard, than a Cheshire cat with its beguiling smile. In the company of his peers Rancid easily slipped on his elegant 'silver tongue' and spoke with quaint eloquence even though his underlying modem was one of intimidation and subtle threat.

And now that he was in Trader's Trove he could lesson his Edwardian pretensions, slide into a more subtle form of pedestrian, and still utilize his same delicate way of prying information from men even if it meant demonstrating the directness of his intent by pulling a knife from his boot sheath and cleaning his nails with its razor sharp blade.

"An Aunt? Mrs. Tumblers? . Hummm," thought Rancid who took his regular table in the far, dark corner where he could spot every drunk entering or leaving. Can't really see the old girl as anyone's Aunt," he thought scurrilously; and it did seem a bit of a stretch to believe that Toad had a relative who had popped in on her as a mystery character at the end of a tawdry detective novel from Kent."

"Putting it all together, if Edna did have a nephew, he would be fully grown into young adulthood. And so the question remained: who in relation to Edna was the boy?" said Rancid again to himself but this time audibly as if cross examining his own inner logic.

"The gardener's son perhaps? No, definitely not . Old Toad would never consider turning the care of his proper garden to someone else; it was his pride, his prize, and Toad spoke more of its finely trimmed rows than he did of his affection for his wife. Certainly not a relative no. But the lad was 'someone'."

Rancid' s fingers found the peanut bowl and grabbed a handful of nuts which he had no intention of eating; instead, he took to laying them in neat order on the table much the same as he lined numbers on a ledger sheet .

Rancid prided himself on being able to keep the issues of his life in orderly fashion and the lining up of peanuts reminded him of how perfectly he had once ordered his toy soldiers. The very discipline of lining up problems and assaulting them one by was the advantage he believed gave him all his life's successes.

Between small gulps from his glass and his modeled ruminations over his new acquaintance Anubis, the door to the Troves opened and darkened with ta figure that looked more like an Arctic yak on two feet than a man who thankfully was Pig, Rancid's degenerate sometime-employee.

The stench of Pig reached Rancid's table before Pig himself. Pig wrestled a seat from a nearby table and sat down as the bartender who had already poured him a pint set it near Pig's side, pinched his nose while walking hurriedly away.

"To ya, Guv'nor," said Pig as he sloshed down the pint in one gulp spilling a quarter of it onto his arm which dripped down to the table.

"Pig my mate, what brings you to such a fine emporium so early in the afternoon?" said Rancid in his usual faux voice as if it had not been he who had arranged the meeting through an intermediary. "I quite expect you would be just rising from sleep having spent most the previous night 'out-and-about' shall we say."

Pig looked up from his empty glass smiling. When Pig smiled there came two carnivorous teeth on either side of his mouth caressing his bottom lip. The greeting volunteered by Rancid was of course filled with sarcasm. Plg was not of any exaggeration the definition of a 'mate'. And Rancid's mentioning of the 'goings on about town' might have been nothing less than extortion of a prominent city official having compromised himself with one of the girls under

Rancid's employment. Or the decapitation of a comrade's head, or burying alive a litter of puppies just for the fun of it.

"Business Gov'nr…" responded Pig who was looking over his shoulder trying to signal the bartender.

"And I needn't ask if the business is a serious one, need I?" asked Rancid of his deleterious deeds.

"Not when some bloke is lining my pockets with the right number of shillings," said Pig with a wink and then looked around for the tender once more.

Rancid had benefited from Pig's criminal skills for many years and knew that Pig was the perfect choice for the follow-up on the Tumblers estate. Pig was, despite personal appearance, odiferous presence and, living an entirely different existence than he, as resourceful and efficacious a criminal as Rancid himself.

"Well Pig, I was rather keen on seeing you today; thought after visiting the pub and not having the pleasure of your company I'd have to track you down to your quiet abode on the river's edge."

"But I came to ya Gov'nor as an angel on a cloud," said Pig fluttering his hand and fingers like a flying entity. This semblance of poetic verse brought forth a belch from Pig as a projectile of froth simultaneously shot from his mouth landing a few inches in front of Rancid as a coagulated ball of mucus.

Rancid wondered if it were all really worth the effort; were there not ample enough to retire on were he to cash in his bonds, sell his several properties (those rat-hole tenements in Liverpool, foreclose the mortgage on the senior retirement housing etc, etc. .; he could purchase a small cottage in Surrey, live the life of a country gentleman, send for a girl from somewhere in Germany uneducated and with few English speaking skills; have the frau clean the cottage, prepare the meals, mend his clothes and be his private pounding mattress at night) ?

Rancid signaled for Daniels who came loaded with more refreshment with which Pig lunged upon. Rancid put several coins down on the table engaging Daniels, "See that my friend here is forever full to the brim," said Rancid jovially.

"Ya leaven' so soon, are ya Gov'nor?" said Pig who's mouth and jaw were covered over in dross as if he had been a horse and run an exhausting race.

"I've business too, Mate," said Rancid rising to his feet. "Wonder Sir, if I might find you in your habitat this time tomorrow? I do need to think a bit more deeply about the project I was considering you for."

"You'll be quite welcome, Gov'nor, long's ya bring your call'en card," a term Pig held synonymous with minted coins, and once again felt the unction to belch out a laugh having used his invented jargon.

Rancid's returned to his townhouse at twilight which in contrast to his scurrilous living habits was surprisingly genteel. The furnishings were of light wood with calm, gentle curves highly polished, understated beige fabric coverings with scrolls designed in floral shapes. The pillows on all the settings were another topic : multiple shapes of bright pastels dancing like fallen petals upon the diadem as if a disgruntled housekeeper was taking out his or her angst for her less than fulfilling sex life.

Over the hearth hung two Stubbs oil paintings which allowed the viewer intimate scenes of mares with their fledgling foals nestled together under huge chestnut trees.

The drawing room walls of Rancid's were stenciled in the current Moroccan motif; intricate curves intertwined and doubling back upon each strand as if they had emotions and forgotten which direction they were originally headed. These designs were shaded in numerous faded colors with multiple values to set them in favorable picturesque style but none so powerful to compete with the overall decorative effect of calm meditation.

Rancid employed a gentleman's gentleman, a certain, Lord Farnsworth by name, (a man who satisfied his base needs at the knocking houses of London's lower end and therefore could not be the person to accuse for flinging pillows about) whose cell door Rancid had jangled free by stuffing multiple pounds in a presiding magistrate's pocket.

Rancid had sought out the 'said' Lord Farnsworth, as a man who owned a reputation in the underworld of commerce by showing great dexterity in the fine arts of forgery, and the ability to unscramble tumblers in safe vaults.

Over the years Rancid utilized his employed Lord for the above mentioned skills and in particular the breaking into wall safes of families' homes he had stayed at as 'honored guest' and had seen what paintings or false partitions they were hidden behind.

Altogether the relation between the two men was that of Rancid calling upon Farnsworth for each and every whim he might be predisposed to and the former jailbird continuing with the liberty of living under the silly affectation of Lordship understanding that any infraction against the relation with Rancid might jettison him back to prison.

Rancid had accumulated for himself the rule over many a mans and womens destinies; Lord Farnsworth being only one nefarious character who owed their their lack of detention in prison but who had simultaneously traded their day to-day freedom to become Rancid's virtual slaves.

"Good evening Sir", said Lord Farnsworth as Rancid scrapped some sort of tar from his right shoe onto the metal grating made for such a purpose which had been cast in metal in the form of a skunk.

Rancid said nothing to his licentious employee in-crime as he stood in the foyer allowing Farnsworth to disrobe his cape and take his top hat with cane.

Rancid briefly looked at the day's mail which had been placed into stacks on a table by the door; news circulars, invoices, personal letters (none), and a stack of legal dictatorial that plague even the most adroit of monsters. Rancid would tend to these items at some later time when he was less traveled and less weary, but for now there was the insistent whisper from a lamentable siren, something half alive, half not dead.

"I will be taking tea in the drawing room," said Rancid to Lord Farnsworth the same as if his gentleman were a shadow of a lamp pole, with Farnsworth responding in the affirmation: "Sir".

Rancid was sitting in his high back with his head tilted to the ceiling and his eyes closed as Farnsworth served the steaming tea accompanied by an ornate silver sifter containing brandy.

Once served and Lord Farnsworth had exited, Rancid allowed himself a moment of humanity by admitting exhaustion for all the mix of machinations he had experienced for the day and breathed a great heave of air.

"My," he thought "and to have gotten so far in this life and still be at the behest of so many minute particulars all needing the attentiveness of a child in the crib".

Rancid filled his tea cup half way and then poured the full of the sifter into the remainder.

With a few sips of the strong mixture he found himself immediately revived.

"And now, again, to the business of the Tumbler's manor," said Rancid to himself as he stretched forth his slipper feet onto silk covered stool and poised his hands together that his fingertips met in an angular arch taught him by his dear mum while he attended Catechism classes.

But before delving further into an attack strategy on The Pulstar, Rancid allowed himself a rare reminisce into the memory of his Mummy and how she lived her early years like an old carpet laid across a stretched rope. And as she was splayed for all her indignities to be exploited, The Divines of the Heavens beat her with brooms as if to cleanse her soul for having the misfortune of being born into the slums of London.

"What great need was there of hers to care for himself, his brothers and sisters?" thought Rancid painfully. While other mothers suffocated their 'passionate accidents' at birth, or surgically removed their children-to-be by prying a button hook up, into their bodies , Madam Rancidimore, Dearest Mum, chose the life of a mother mouse surrounding herself with multiple needy mouths to fill.

"How was she able to provide him and his siblings with the meager gruel in their bowls each night? And what exactly was her 'job' that not only earned her sixpence but , often time earned her bruises and cuts on her body as well? And to what worth was it for her to see six little mice hovelled together under one blanket feeding off each others warmth displaying teeth marks and scratches given them by each other or nibbling mice while she was away?

"Life is severe is it not? thought Rancid who was unawares how strongly each joint of his fingers were testing his ability to endure the discomfort of arthritis in his hands .

"Would it not be wonderful could I reach to the past and bring Me' Mother along to live here at Hampstead Heath?" Rancid who was so unused to having a kind thought about anyone, was unawares that he was drifting on a long paragraph of how he would set up a fine room for his mother to sleep in with the finest of linens on her bed, the best of foods, the most elegant of gowns; have her arm woven through his as they entered a grand theater and every person there could see that he, the Hideous Mr. Rancid was not such a bad chap at all while the care he showed for his Mum would redeem him from all past and future life's digressions?

And just then, as if a new planet in the heavens was first observed by an earthly astronomer, the veil of tears that washes the lives of us all, welled up for one brief expression, as a singular tear dislodged itself from the corner of Rancid's eye tracing a path like a small snowball cascading down an icy slope, down to the chin of his pock marked face

Whatever gains had been made for the cause of compassionate humanity, what with reminiscing about the sorrows of childhood, and the flow of that singular tear upon his ruddy skin, were all quickly dispelled by Rancid for what he considered an embarrassed himself of his own reputation and dispelled the moment as if it had wafted away like a bad rumor from a card room.

Rancid dabbed the tell-tale droplet away from his face, and the surugging his shoulders took in a deep breath and turned his mind again to the task of destroying the lonely life of Edna Tumbler's.

Rancid woke the following morning with the perfect solution for the dilemma of securing information written in Toad's diary and ledgers, his safe, and essentially the Tumblers fortunes.

True, it would be a complicated contrivance set against Madame Tumblers, thus paving the necessity for her being committed to an asylum.

Once secured away she might even find a perverse joy acting the role of a favored matriarch once removed, luring imbecilic gentlemen to chase her about as if she were a belle-of-the-ball, thought Rancid laughingly.

Madame Tumblers had led a charmed life as far as Rancid could surmise: born into a family of means; marrying a disputed 'man' of valor, one who himself had untold pound notes, and silver reserves tagged onto his name the day he escaped the confines of the womb.

This seemed as good as an excuse to wipe away any guilt Rancid may have for banishing Edna to the asylum. Yes, even Rancid had a touch of conscious left in his soul which he relished; not as one might assume, acting as a symbol for charity, but as a prompt to him that caution for the potential perils he might encounter any particular day.

Edna was merely an obstacle; but, then there was the other issue: the boy child; and again

He asked himself "who was he really?" There was a certain intangible air about the child, Anubis; a feeling that the boy was, (how could one say?) "fleeting".

The child was something like a person who was there and yet, not present at all; a person so attentive to the moments events and yet, so distracted as if he were living in another world altogether. And though Rancid had encountered innumerable curious personalities in the streets and receiving rooms of London, he found himself at a loss to put his finger on an identity for this particular lad and his curious demeanor, and the extravagance for calling himself "Anubis" .

Rancid was sitting up in bed at this mornings hour of further contemplation, his serving table across his lap ; his specified menu of boiled eggs, toast, and tea which Lord Farnsworth served him every morning at half past seven.

Rancid never found it convenient to change his base routines. There were so many business issues to configure with everyday, things of such complexity, that not having to think about what would be new on the breakfast plate somehow came as a welcomed respite from all of the other items.

On he thought, examining every possible angle with which to accomplish his tasks while his jaw bone snapped steadily upon the food like the clicking hands of his time piece.

And then there came the expected, gentle knock upon Rancid's door, the reminder from Lord Farnsworth of the long corridor Rancid would walk that day and the manifold number of doors he would have to darken.

"Indeed, Sir," responded Rancid with the same level of enthusiasm an actor in his room gives with the five minutes preceding his entrance into life's drama.

CHAPTER III: PART THREE

None of the doors Rancid was to darken that day were as foreboding as the one the cabbie left him off in front of and the dirt path which led to Pig's home.

Rancid could see a steady stream of smoke rising above a clump of bushes indicating Pig was certainly burrowing in his wooden shack which lay on the banks of the Thames River a mile or so south of the capitol.

In his sober moments Pig enjoyed sharing his wit, and what he considered far-reaching humor. There was a sign half hanging from a post near the front entrance door with painted with letters vaguely discernible reading: "Welcome Fiends".

When Rancid tapped the front door with his cane and a bark as loud as two mastodons whose tails had been stepped upon simultaneously bellowed from inside yelling: "I've got me' knife and I'll' cut'en yer innards out with it, so helps me Abra'am!"

"I say," said Rancid jovially covering up his uncertainty about the state of Pig's alcoholic induced condition, "It's me Old Boy: Rancid. I say, I've come for that little chat we promised one another; I have brought my 'calling card'," he said knowing that no matter what level of consumption Pig was in, the mention of "money" would be enough to sober him up.

Rancid could hear Pig stumble and curse and eventually try his hand at the knob. "Rancid!" shouted Pig as he flung open the door while throwing out his arms in a theatrical gesture reserved on stages for that of the father receiving the Prodigal Son home.

A blast of air shot out from Pig's mouth and hit Rancid in the face as if it were a dead horse carcass thrown. "Come en' Lad, come on', said Pig to Rancid making an effort to embrace his "mate" in a gesture of mutual brotherhood. Rancid barely missed the embrace by ducking and then stepping lively into Pig's pigsty.

Pig slammed the door and followed Rancid into his 'receiving room' which consisted of one chair and one apple box to sit upon. "For yu' Lad, said Pig reaching for a half drained bottle of port holding it out to Rancid.

"You are so kind, my good man," said Rancid holding up both hands, "but I certainly cannot

At such an early hour Mate; the wife would smell it out of me before I opened the garden gate." "Ahhh, tesk, said Pig, "ya' anit' got no wifen, aeir ya?"

"Didn't say she was mine now did I? Some other blokes; let him pay for her wedding gown and suppers I always say," related Rancid with a look of perversity .

And with this tale about infidelity Pig let out another of his ghastly howls and then buckled at the knees putting his hands on them to keep from falling over.

On Pig laughed for upwards of a full minute wheezing and sneezing trying to catch his breath. "Ats' a good un' Rancid", said Pig when he was able to stand more or less upright. "Make the other bloke buy the bat er' dresses!" and with this said, Pig ladled out another geyser of smelt, and ore in Rancid's direction that was so powerful Rancid pulled out his handkerchief and flattened it against his face. Pig again buckled at his knees so violently that Rancid grabbed Pig by the shoulders and led him backwards to a mangled high back chair plunking him down.

"Sir!" said Rancid loudly. "Sir!" said Rancid again shaking Pig. "Sir, I am here on business. As I have said I did bring my calling card; in fact I brought a number of calling cards." Rancid forthwith dug into his inner coat pocket and whipped out a wad of currency waving it like a fan across Pig's face.

Magic! Pig's face contorted; like a train coming to a station and at the last minute having to change tracks and Pig's countenance straightened into sobriety.

"Don't mind if I do, Colonel," said Pig in his perfectly broken King's English while reaching out to grab the paper.

"Only half Mate; remember?" said Rancid pulling part of the cash away and shoving it back into his coat. "Half today and the other half when you bring me the information I need."

"Yu'll ave' yer' information Gov'nor; once't you tell me what it is I will be seeken."

"There is a boy."

"A package ya mean; to be delivered to wha' address?"

"I don't need a boy-package now," said Rancid. "I need you to go to an address and see if you can find out the identity of the child. I have to know who the lad is; who he belongs to."

"E's a lad, Mate," said Pig with a faltering, fatigued laugh. (Not his best joke of the day to be sure). Wha' difference does it make?" And then Pig's eyes twinkled. "An illegitimate of someone in govn-mnt!" This would not be the first 'hidden' child some official had created and was keeping in secret family situation and Pig had brokered into a blackmail position on behalf of his contracted employer.

Pig reached for an open can of beans and dug two of his fingers in for a quick treat. He lifted the mixture out and placed the glob into his mouth licking his fingers with great relish before repeating the action.

Rancid observed Pig's 'quaint' dining habit and thought to himself how much more Pig lived

up to his name than any other character that he had known .

Pig angled a look up to Rancid well aware of his employer's feelings towards him and licked the second portion of beans from his fingers with more sensual delirium than the first.

Pig belched deeply and then took a great swig of his bourbon. He wiped his mouth and belched once more, "'it the spot ya' might say," said Pig with a nasty smile.

"Don't let me keep ya from goin on ' bout the lad, Gov'nor. You was say'in ya' want's me to just look in on the lad ; not steal em'?"

"That's correct , my friend, Pig. The Widow to whom I will be referring you to was more than just a bit unnerved when the child walked into the room," said Rancid with a vague look on his face and raising his eyes to Pig's ceiling which had mold on it due to a large circular formation caused by a water leak. "There is something strange about that relation; very strange indeed," recounted Rancid.

"Well en' which was marked," said Pig holding out his hand with bean residue "like always I am sure you ave' the information."

Rancid reached into a pocket in his trousers producing a slip of paper. On the top of the paper

was the written address of the Pulstar Manor (Rancid had written this information with his left hand - he being right handed- in the event the note was confiscated by the authorities who would find it impossible to trace back to him). Below the address was a map drawn by another of Rancid's assistants with numerous details of roads, back alleyways, gates and possible entrances to the manor.

Rancid allowed himself an inward grin of pride. Lord Farnsworth was undoubtedly the man with the highest profile directly enslaved by Rancid and then the list steadily declined into numerous other categories.

There were prostitutes (some of them quite fetching to look upon) who could seduce regents of the State; thugs to wring the necks of shopkeepers for protection money, and for items concerning specialties such as surveillance of locations and delineated maps, Rancid employed his cartographer, a one Mr. Sims, a frail man he kept on a leash with droplets of heroin.

"You'll find once again all the details pertinent to the success of your mission," said Rancid who was fitting his coat and cane for departure.

"I must be off, my good man," said Rancid tipping his hat with the ball end of the cane and moved in the direction of the door.

Pig had finished counting the money given him and while reaching again for his bottle of bourbon thought how easy it would be to crash the container across the back of Rancid's head and relieve his employer of the remainder of the money and his finely measured leather boots. But poking out through the air in the room there rose between the two men the same silent

language understood by sleeping dogs. Look at the dog long enough and it will raise

its head and bare its teeth. There is no scientific explanation for such phenomenon but the one who does the staring is soon reminded of the proverb to: 'let sleeping dogs lie'. And this was why Pig remained in his seat with his vile thoughts as Rancid went out , his cane gripped ferociously in his fist .

CHAPTER V

SLAYING OF THE INNOCENTS

It was a typical winter morning in the heart of London and the Pulstar Manor was encased with thick fog like a dainty foot placed with care into a silk slipper. Starring from the back porch window Isabella could only imagine the place of the bramble bush and all of her former adventures and how they lingered before her as if they were a story incomplete .

"My, how years do travel in the memory" thought Isabella as she found herself on the eve of yet another January birthday wondering once again what she would give herself in this the celebration of her twelfth?

Isabella put on her sandals much to the scorn of her mother's caution about the sore throat she had carried all that week previous.

Isabella's purpose was to go roundabout to the plants and pots in the trellis house and tend to their arrangements which she was sure were in disorder due to their long neglect. Trimming here and there and perhaps even repotting a few bulbs she relished the feel of the lush grains of soil caressing her skin and the remembrance of her of times in Toad's tutelage.

There would be no way to coerce Dinaha to corne out with her into the cold and no way she would listen to any more entreaties from Edna whom by this time was instructed to call her daughter exclusively, Anubis and so (Isabella) Anubis Rose left Edna and Dinah to warm themselves by the hearth and thrill to the tunes of a Mendelsohn symphony. Anubis had developed the habit of removing her sandals before walking onto the Pulstar Manor's cold, garden ground and tip-toed gingerly upon the colder still, round cement blocks that led to the trellis

.

The trellis had not been trimmed as was Toad's method when the seasons changed from warm to winter. Toad was dead by that delegated time, and Anubis forehead and cheeks were greeted with the tickling of many limp pedals when she pushed her way through the door.

Anubis quite expected to hear Toad's voice (a voice that was so much more different from its tone when he first woke in the morning). In the trellis Toad spoke as if his words were precious glass formations with the need for being arranged perfectly on a menagerie shelf.

"And this shall go over here my Sweet Pea," said Toad taking hold of his daughter's hands as she clasped onto a flower pot and she, wondering at its plants succulent aroma would ask what genus it originated from or was it indeed a hybrid? Toad then took most special care to help his daughter with the identification of the various plants as if she was an initiate into a religious cult.

But alas, Toad was not with his careful words this day and Anubis felt very, very alone. Anubis began digging into the soil barrel and finding the correct bulbs to align, trimming the

dead leaves, pulling weeds, up rooting and potting, watering and even talking with the plants, Anubis felt she had been almost two hours about her horticulture tasks, all the while not

giving a single thought for Edna nor the furry lap-warmer Dinah. And while she fashioned every pot in its respective place, and crafted all the trimmings, she began to feel as if she were in another world, a place far, far away from the Pulstar Manor much the same as if she were once again a princess in a fairy tale land.

And just then Anubis bent her head and angled her ears thinking she heard a stirring outside the trellis, and that perhaps the noise had come from a ghost to her from somewhere in Toad's realm.

Anubis had never known the feeling of fright, having been so cared for in her loving home and in full command of the goings on of her dream world that she did not know she actually was feeling afraid.

Anubis did though, conjure up a similar scent to the one she smelled now and that would have been the time she was introduced to the hideous Mr. Rancid. Anubis crouched down below a potting table taking a deep breath to see if that same scent accompanied was coupled with that noise.

There the sound came again and Anubis put her hand to her mouth to remind herself not to scream and give away her hiding place. Anubis focused her concentration in the direction of the door but knew ghosts could come into the trellis without using the door or even a window.

And then the door did part but, only by a few inches which was just the width needed to enable

two incredibly cute bunnies the room they needed to squeeze in through. "Baron Nelson!" cried Anubis, "and Lady Emma!" Oh my goodness I thought I would never have seen the two of you again."

Anubis rubbed her eyes and cheeks with the back of his hands and bent down to her two friends who moved with great rapidity knowing that they would be warmly snuggled.

Anubis began talking in a stream of sentences not even taking so much as a breath going from story to story about her acquisition of Dinah and the death of Toad and how his fainting had caused the flooding in the King Crabs hall and how she, Anubis had permanently changed her name (at least for the permanent now) and wondered if she should begin reconstructing the Court?

But then she also expressed concern that if she would go to all that trouble she might find herself alone in her coronation clothing bemoaning the favored days of her greatness while acting as Princess Isabella, and how now she would sit alone looking very foolish; a potentate with no one to 'tate' to.

And when Anubis did inhale a breath she noticed something absolutely marvelous . "Lady Emma , you are with child ! Why this is wonderful ! Congratulations to you both," said Anubis snuggling the bunnies closer still.

The three reunited friends took turns playing catch-up for the lost year or so from their last seeing one another until Baron Nelson broke the triad and took to the task of gathering food .

Lady Emma and Isis talked vigorously about the arrival of Lady Emma ' s children , how many offspring she thought she might be carrying and what if any names she had chosen; how many girl bunnies and how many boys?

In time the fog rose and gave way to a blooming afternoon and the two ladies followed Baron Nelson by making their way out of the trellis house and walking about the garden stopping just briefly by the entrance leading into the thicket that once housed the Court of Forty.

While Anubis, Baron Nelson and Lady Emma shared their reflections about the high adventures they had once lived, an indistinct form passed in the bushes along the east end gate that neither of them had necessarily seen but somehow made all of three feel squeamish .

"We are never alone on this planet," said Baron Nelson breaking the silence that had corne over them. "Ghosts from past lives , perhaps from the future . . . we are but poor creatures and form the most part horribly incapable of understanding our Lord's machinations . "

"Well versed, my Love," said Lady Emma as she sunk her head into Baron Nelson's arm.

"You see why I fall deeper in love with him every day, don't you, Anubis?"

"What woman could ever resist a poet?" said Anubis having recalled Toads teaching about the falling away of many hearts to the muse Kroisos, the nude youth who plucked the emotions of Grecian women with his harp and his lyrical words.

Young Anubis, Baron Nelson and his beloved better half Emma talked and played well into the late afternoon, having taken a lunch of crackers, and bits of lettuce leaves while sitting on Anubis' calico colored bed covering which she had gone into gather from her bedroom. And when they had finished their meal, Baron Nelson excused himself and retrieved a lengthy cigar from a pouch on the underside of his coat .

Baron Nelson wandered far enough away that the smoke from his cigar would not affect the two ladies and with a distance assured to them that they could speak on any topic women talk about without consideration that he might hear .

Lady Emma climbed up into Anubis' lap telling her friend about being an expectant mother basking in repose as Anubis petted her lovingly and she whispered her private thoughts . And of course Anubis responded with loving compassion for her, remembering after all, Lady Emma was a beast of nature and all the more helpless in the presence of a mammal the size of herself.

Baron Nelson allowed his mind to wander aimlessly as he walked the parameter of the Polstar acreage never not far from the ladies in the event they might have an emergency encounter with a scavenger cat.

He tried to imagine himself as a proud father of (how many had Lady Emma thought nestled in her stomach?) ; no matter, he would embrace each of them.

"Can't wait to see you again my Love," said Lady Emma as Anubis bent down and rubbed noses with her.

"Something like heaven," said Anubis to herself as the bunnies bounded away into the underbrush.

"The homecoming is always more sweet than the dream."

The furry couple turned to wave farewell and then disappeared into the bramble. They found the trail to the base of the oak tree where they had come into the Pulstar estate which was near the East gate.

"Wasn't this just the most wonderful afternoon," said Lady Emma as she lay her head upon Baron Nelson's shoulder. But Baron Nelson was only half listening.

Had he been commanding a frigate in any of the ocean waters the Baron would have known how to maneuver his wife and himself away from what he sensed as a present and great danger. He certainly could not ask Emma to run to escape in her prenatal condition, and yet he should have done something instead of nothing.

For in the wink of a mammal's eye, Pig reached out of the shadowy undergrowth throwing a burlap sack upon both bunnies. Baron Nelson and Lady Emma were so shocked with fright that neither of them could find the voice to say a final "I love you".

Once they were secured in the sack Pig tied a sailors knot upon them and skipped away laughing thinking about the information he had gained about the boy and his good fortune for trapping his evening meal.

Part Two:

"Ees' a-collard."

"What did you say?" asked Rancid incredulously.

"Ye e'ared me mate; I said es' a-collared. Ye' seen im' , now don't tell's me es' ough't." "I saw him of course; I was the one put you to finding out about him."

"Ya seen es ' not quite pitch-black but sure enough es ' a-collared. No two ways bout it."

"Impossible! He had red hair."

"Must'a been the light, mate; an' yer drink'en a ' course." And with this deduction Pig laughed himself "a good-un".

Pig was sitting like a king upon a throne . His King Edwardian coat was blown open and his never washed white -now turned eternally soiled brownshirt sprouted a length of brass buttons half of which were lost while engaging in tavern room brawls . Pig's feet were stretched out upon the apple crate with one boot off, and the other dangling on his toes . Pig was drunk. Not that Pig was ever sober , but Pig was unusually drunk holding a large goblet of whisky in one hand and a rabbit leg drumstick in the other.

"Care's for bit' 0' bunny, Govni'r ," said Pig stupidly.

Pig with a mouth full of pulse and wine that mixed together i n one cheek and spilled "No thank , you, I do not have the appetite" said Rancid with more sincerity than he had spoken in the last decade. "But I must press you friend about this matter of the boy being a 'collared'. How on earth did you corne to so sure a notion?"

"Easy gov'nir; seen im' widt' both me eyes; same as you." Pig thought about what he had just said and wondering in his drunken state if he had just said what he had just said, and then when he concluded he had, he said "widt' me eyes, jus' same as you." And feeling in himself that he had uttered something of a profound statement (a veritable proverb) Pig smiled again and let out a boisterous laugh projecting food across his unwashed shirt of missing brass buttons.

"I see," said Rancid contemplating whether he should shoot Pig in his fat face and keep the remainder of the money he had promised to pay him?

"Ya' see Govir' I'm think'en you seen im' in an ouse'; I seen im' outside in the sun', make's sense, don't it Mr. Rancid, sir?"

"Perhaps," said Rancid. Rancid took in a deep breath as Pig tore off another rabbit leg. Pig held out the leg for Rancid who put his hand up in a negative response. "C'mon Gov'nir, got another four legs afer' this un."

Rancid waved his hand again and said "Is there anything else you noticed about the boy; was there anything in his speech you picked up; any movement: anything?"

"Well un' Gov'nir I kin tell ye he's a bit tetched," said Pig who pointed to his head indicating Anubis, whom we still remember is Isabella Rose the girl with the enormous green eyes.

"How did you come to this conclusion about the boy being crazy?" said Rancid whose hand had come to rest on the butt of the revolver hidden in his coat pocket.

"He's goin' round talk'in to im' self all after noon. Crazy I says. Play'en blinds-mans-bluff widt a couple invisible bunnies, talk'in with dem' as if they's chillen, and they warnt even real."

"Playing games and talking to himself is nothing so unusual; heavens! He's a child. All children have make-believe friends. I had them when I was a child. Altogether they were a lot more trustworthy than my so called friends today."

"Suit yer self Gov'nir," said Pig stuffing his mouth with the entire rabbit leg and guzzling the remainder of the goblet contents. "Another crazy collared' e' is . Not'en so unusual. Seen lots of em' down the ship yard. Always talk'en to emselves; singen Gospel songs and all. Goin' on and on' as if en' they're messengers un' God or sum' fen."

Anubis was unspeakably overjoyed at the reunion she had had with her two friends. She hardly felt the water run over her as she sat in the tub and poured lemon oil down about her head. Once the bath was complete, and once she was dried and sitting upon her bed propped up like always against the headboard Anubis wanting to go into a restful meditation, instead startled as she heard a krinkling noise behind the pillow supporting her back.

She reached her hand around and discovered the noise came from a lavender colored envelope, much larger than you could find on the curio shelves of Hastings Row. And inside this overly large envelope was a single, silvery colored rectangle page written in a cursive style that one would expect came from the hand of a seasoned scribe; one who sat at the footstool of a king, or a prince and had taken down every word to transcribe every utterance as if they would be sealed and sent heavenward.

And the page read:

"Dear Princess Isabella, all seems lost! The eldest son of the King Crab is on the move. After the war he gathered many of the straggling forces who escaped your armies grasp and they have, with other new recruits, amassed an armada of their own which is equal to if not greater than his father's. With the greatest humiliation and exhaustive plea, we again beg your intervention on behalf of all those innocent souls who wish for nothing but the chance to live in harmony and peace. Most Sincerely Yours,

The Queen of the Seals

Anubis sat stunned. She felt she could almost say within herself: "Who is this Princess Isabella and what troubles must she endure again simply because she was resident of Pulstar Manor and the recipient of this request?"

But Anubis could not say this, for in reality she was Princess Isabella and the identity disguise of being Anubis she had assumed for a quiet term of retirement was nothing she could wear as long as her friends lives, and liberties were threatened.

There is no hindering a true friend who wishes to come to your rescue when you request their help and, Anubis showed the depth of her concern when she jumped from her bed and ran to the clothes closet before you could say: "clothes closet".

Princess Isabella was fully revived in her imagination by the somewhat musty aroma of the closet which held her gun powdery, soot-infused jacket, pants, vest and helmet of her warrier days.

Isabella lifted her coat off its hanger and was reminded of how heavy and stiff it was due to the special meshing that made it resilient to shrapnel.

"Now what to do about my hair?" thought Isabella as she reached up to grab her helmet which with the level of its weight and the accumulative moisture in the closet had attached itself to the shelf as if it were glued. There was a popping sound when Isabella forced it away from its setting and when she placed it on it seemed as if either her head had gained mass or the helmet had shrunken.

"My hair .... " What of my hair? Certainly it flows as a regal mane across my head and down my shoulders."

In truth Isabella's hair had only grown four inches during the three quarter year furlough acting as Anubis and her bangs hung no more than three quarter inches down her forehead; there was no hint of a curl, no wave, and in all honesty, nothing that would help Princess Isabella appear "Grand!"

The days of short hair had passed. Edna had instilled in her daughter that a Grand Dame of English royalty would never appear in public with less than a show piece upon her pate. "Yes", said Isabella as she struggled with the placement of the helmet on her head. "I must look the part of a Princess;" said Isabella talking as if she were scolding the child whom was she. "I must be Grand for my subjects, someone they will follow into battle, someone (dare she say it?): "Someone they will worship!"

PART III

Trader's Trove was jumping to the intensity of the neighbor's cat whose tail someone had tied firecrackers to and ignited, and every bit as loud. The ship workers had just come up the lane having watched restlessly as a minor city official and a few other incompetent officiates participate in the traditional cracking of a bottle of champagne on the hull of a large, newly finished barge before the support pilings were knocked down and it slid back and into the Thames for its maiden voyage.

"You smell like an overcooked pork roast," came a voice from the back table in the tavern. The

comment was directed to a man standing motionless who looked as if he had been vomited from the bowels of the earth.

"No trouble I am hoping?"

"Not from where I stand," said Lord Farnsworth who waited for the motion from Rancid's hand before he took a seat. "And," said Rancid sipping his ale with the casualness of a man with nothing on his mind but taxes, but was taken in thought about the probabilities of being hung from the gallows for his authorizing Pig's murder.

"The bobbies can search until the day a man walks the craters of the moon."

"And what, if anything extra, might you be expecting for your services?"

"You pay me well as it is," said Farnsworth. I see no reason for gratuity," and then looked over his shoulder to see if an ale were forthcoming.

And what about his stash?" said Rancid his two eyes, even in the dim, smoke filled room looked as if they were drilling holes through Lord Farnsworth's brain.

"Stash?" asked Farnsworth ignorantly. Rancid made the slightest shift in his posture. "Stash," said Farnsworth as if Rancid had just cocked a pistol. "Right!" A bead of sweat trailed perceptively across Farnsworth's brow and down one side of his face.

"Actually our man had several bags of coins and a few odds and ends; silver candelabras , watches; the like. Will you be wanting a full accounting?" Rancid answered with a patented turn of the head.

"The money is mine of course. You keep the other items; you may want them as heirlooms if you fail your next assignment."

Daniel's came to the table with two pints of ale billowing over and cascading to the floor as he shuffled. "Sorry Gov'nir," he said to Rancid with a bow. "Blokes won't leh' me serv'ce me finest cust'mers."

"I shall always return to your fine establishment Daniels; nothing so fine an emporium

as you have built!" said Rancid in an energetic and wholly gratuitous voice . Daniel's face lifted at the cheekbones with a wide grin and as he bent again in servitude he looked sideways at Lord Farnsworth.

Daniels reaching out his right hand "Don't bel'eve I've ad' the pleasure." Farnsworth put forward his hand with hesitation simultaneously turning his head so his face would be covered in the shadows.

"This would be one of my surveyors Mr. Daniels: Roberts," said Rancid. He was just up the lane on a job; a bit of land soon for public sale; I want to get in on the bid early."

"You always was a smart un', Mr. Rancid," said Daniels pointing his index finger to his temple as if he were a school master coaxing students to recite in wrote.

Just then a fight broke out between several of the patrons and Daniels, bowing politely at the waist said, "pleasure ta ' meet ya Mr. Rob'rts ," and he took a black-jack from his apron while he headed in the direction of the fight .

"The Irish," said Rancid with disdain, "should have wiped them off the face of the earth decades ago. Allow them into a civilized society and look what you've got; yet another brawl."

"My mother and grandmother were Irish," said Lord Farnsworth in a low, bitter voice Rancid chose not to hear the comment and in a few moments when the brawl settled down (Mr. Daniels used his black-jack to crack open the skull of the Irish instigator), set into the design for Lord Farnsworth's next assignment.

"I have thought of a good title for the roll you will be playing on my behalf, Lord Farnsworth," said Rancid in the tone of a lion tamer indicating that if Farnsworth did not jump to the crack of his whip that a man standing just outside the circus bars would shoot the beast dead. "We shall call it," he said merrily, "The Actor's Life for Me."

"Excuse me Sir , am I to understand I will be performing on stage?"

 "Oh, you thespians ; so melodramatic. Not literally the stage Lord Farnsworth; indeed I have something so much more challenging for you than allowing you to waste your talents on some bit-part in a Gilbert-Sullivan toe tap , sing along ."

"No, my good man, I mean the real stage; real life acting! A roll any Shakespearian actor would salivate for in his cross-dressing boots to play."

"I don't know that I've ever related Sir, that I have had a bit of stage training; quite a fare share actually," said Farnsworth immediately believing in his ability to fulfill any role Rancid set out.

"You don't say?" said Rancid with a look of awe . "I would expect I am the biggest appreciators of your multiple talents; but a certifiable thespian; I am one more time impressed and intrigued."

"I began acting when I was a child," said Farnsworth assured he had a captivated audience.

"Did some singing and acting with my older brothers on the street corners. Eventually I tried out for my first theater production. In time I took lessons to become a better actor; I built sets, and I even fell in love with an actress. Perhaps I have told you I once orchestrated an acting troupe in prison?"

"We were the 'Flying Imbeciles'? Actually the play was all about mocking the prison warden and the guards. I wrote and directed it ."

"And .," said Rancid who was signaling for another round of ale for Lord Farnsworth whose eyes had dropped slightly back into his head while reaching for what apparently were his days touching the face of fame.

"And what, Sir?"

"Well, my good man, how were you received; did the warden and the imbecilic guards catch on?"

"Nothing to catch on to Sir. I escaped the day it was to be performed. The entire idea of the play was a distraction; 'in confusion there will be profits,'" said Lord Farnsworth straightening In his chair as if he were embarking on a moral lecture. "And the prize was my freedom."

"I commend you upon your inventiveness," said Rancid following along as if he were not thinking The Lord Farnsworth's sudden, pompous reverie was a nauseating bit of overacting in itself. ("There's a place in the grave for you along-side Pig and you'll fill it soon enough, Lord Farnsworth") thought Rancid as the ends of his mouth pushed deep into his cheeks in a false gesture of delight while Daniels arrived with two more ales and Farnsworth went on about his acting 'career'.

"Bit a' brawl," said Daniels apologetically bowing again as he placed the pints on the table . "Appens whenever the Irish comes. They're the brawlen ' type. Ope ' they didn't disturb your conva'sation Sir."

"Rather entertaining, altogether," said Rancid . "Will I be seeing a surcharge for the performance on my tab?"

The tavern owner let out a bellow. "You are the clever un, now aint ya now, Govnir?" said Daniels lifting his index to his temple again. " You always was a smart ' un," he said and scurried back to his duties.

After the men had received their drinks Rancid reached out his glass to clink his mate's Lord Farnsworth. "Now on to the task," whispered Rancid leaning forward his head as he had seen acted in the play Treasure Island when the pirates conspired about buried booty.

Rancid was betting Lord Farnsworth had also seen London's current, most popular play Treasure Island and how quite unexpectedly he may delight in the idea of himself being cast in the role of a pirate.

And sure enough he had. Rancid observed Lord Farnsworth, as similar in body pose as if he were auditioning for one of the pirate roles and looking briefly over both his shoulders and then adjusting his coat collar, crooked his neck forward and spoke in conspiratorial overtones while winking his eyes in evil collusion.

Isabella had not laughed for so many long months that it hurt to feel happy again as she recalled rolling on the ground that morning with Lady Emma and her husband.

And here again she was enjoying herself for the second time since the flooding of King Clams fortress and the Court of Forty as she stood in Edna's boudoir while Edna placed on Isabella's head a variety of wigs.

"And this one I recall I wore to my good friend Patricia Anne's so called 'Dark Opera' Ball," said Edna placing a flowing, black wig onto Isabella's head.

"It feels a bit heavy Mum," said Isabella who thought of the crown she would soon be wearing and then once onto battle would have to replace the crown with a helmet.

"Then we shall try this one," said Edna placing a ravishing red mantel of real hair (no doubt shorn by a young lady while weeping great tears, that she might sell the lengths to payoff some debt and pay for a gift that she might give to someone she loved) upon her daughter's head as if it was a symbol of coronation.

"I quite like it Mother," said Isabella as she fingered the ruby-rose strands through her fingers. "But I would also I would like to try on the others as well."

And so the two ladies sat in the boudoir, primping and pulling, combing and brushing; utilizing hairpins, adjusting barrettes, and fashioning ribbons for the entire remains of the day.

In the late hours Isabella could see her mother was faltering to exhaustion, and felt for herself that she had given as much attention to the aggrandizement of her own image as was needed, and inclined upon the red wig made from real hair.

"You look extraordinary Princess Isabella, said Edna who had been told about the visit from the two rabbits, the urgent note from the Queen of the Seals and the necessity for the now 'Isabella' to help her friends.

"I am much too old to go rummaging through bramble bushes dear," said Edna in response to Isabella's request that her mother attend the reconvening of the Court of Forty.

"But I shall support you Princess Isabella, and be as loyal as any of your other servants." "Mother, I shall never consider you a servant. You are my best friend," said Isabella in a light, fainting tone knowing in her heart that she held her mother in just slightly more esteem than that of a toadstool .

"Then I shall be your biggest supporter, I shall pray for you without ceasing, cook your meals, and have new sheets on your bed every time you return from your duties."

"But Mother, you already do all of these things and I respect you for it," said Isabella with false sincerity before going forth to reside upon her throne once again.

Before convening to the Court of Forty, Isabella's request of Edna was that she help her with one more thing and this would be the setting her face with makeup. This Isabella explained would evoke much the same an essence as the ruler Queen Elizabeth had done for herself.

"But I shall not cover your face in what amounted to Elizabeth becoming a plaster cast," said Edna who related that England's queen in the fourteenth century had so much makeup on her face that at the time of death it was removed, and found to be a mixture that weighed altogether three pounds.

SLAYING OF THE INNOCENT : Part II, Continued

"Goodbye my dear," called out Edna from the glass doors to Isabella who was accompanied by Dinah and stuffed like a lunch bucket under her arm.

"Goodbye mother," returned Isabella who had hold of one of Dinah's' paws and used it like a fan to wave the salutation.

"You'll be back for tea time ... ?" asked Edna who very well knew that the question was superfluous considering her princess daughter would not be home until she had vanquished her enemies.

Isabella remained motionless as she sat upon her throne while her many subjects filed in and took their seating or standing positions. Two crows gleaming with the deepest ivory black colored feathers stood at either side of Princess Isabella ready to give an accounting of everyone present.

Dinah, never having been in the Court of Forty was busy sniffing about the entire interior moving in and out of the colonnades, darting under foot, claw and wing of the many bodies which filled the court until she came face to beak with an enormous owl. This owl had flown in from the land of 'Another-Never-Never-Land', a valley somewhere tucked away in the Inkel Mountains of Prussia. His name was Sir Brandenburg Clausentine III and because he had flown in straight formation and not stopped once in a seventeen day and night flight he was utterly famished with hunger.

Sir Brandenburg Clausentine III was a gentle bird in full control of his natural, animal tendencies, for had he not been, he would have been a dark shadow falling from the sky while Dinah lounged in the Pulstar Manor garden and finding razor sharp talons piercing her skin before she passed-out with terror and pain.

This face-to-beak encounter with Sir Brandenburg Clausentine III sent Dinah scurrying back to Isabella's throne where she jumped up onto

Isabella's lap and nestled deeply into the covering of her mistress's warrior coat.

"The Court of Forty" shall come to order," called Rambletomb Rat, a cute yet sturdy looking rodent from the left bank underbrush of the Thames river near to where the immense curve which broke the rivers straight path shuttling it outward in the direction of the sea, was leaning over a sheaf of papers attached to a wooden lectern.

"All rise, and of those who are already standing, let us give acknowledgment to our great Princess Isabella Rose that we may thank her for her willingness to participate in this unfortunate none the less urgent situation."

With this preamble of Rambletomb Rat the entire court responded resoundingly with a reserved level of applause and several chirps from the birds and a noticeably deep "hoot" from Sir Clausenstein III.

And once the curtailed appreciation stopped the Court settled into a hum of expectation for what their Princess would say. Isabella's faux hair dangled in couplets and ringlets across her brow, her shoulders, and midway down her back framing her face and spread out as an elegant cape around her.

Isabella went right to business thanking all those who had shown subjection to her Court, her office, and for the timeliness of every beings arrival on this day.

"And for those of you have come from especially long distances," said Isabella with her eyes to the right side of the Court where Sir Clausenstein III stood, and then dipped her head in recognition of his many days flight, (and he in response bowing his head ever so lightly; closing his eyes for a length that was far longer than an owl ever shuts his lids (unless in a deep sleep), my great regards for your obeisance to my decree.

"My decree ," said one of the crows under his breath and to himself. Isabella commenced her declaration of war-talk and how she intended to vanquish the enemy by showing no mercy to those who had broken the treaty she had forced the King Clam to "grovel and to sign".

And after the preliminary goings-over of the logistical data; the transport ships, the artillery, once again, the reconnaissance ocean mammals both porpoise and whale and the aviary patrols Princess Isabella gave direction that each grouping of soldiers huddle around their respective chief officers and synchronize their specific strategies .

Princess Isabella motioned for Roquefort Rat to approach her throne and as he flopped up the stair embankment with his tremendously large feet and lent his tremendously oversized ears to Isabella's cupped hand she whispered something that made Roquefort Rat's eyebrows arch and his eyes wink with disbelief.

"It appears my servant M. Rat" said Isabella ln a conspiratorial voice "we have a spy within our midst."

"Can we be certain, M'Lady?" whispered Roquefort Rat incredulously.

"I am your Princess, scribe, do you doubt my words?"

"No M'Lady", said Roquefort Rat aware that the collar of his ruffled shirt was riddled with a sudden flood of sweat and sticking to his hairy body.

"Then you will do as I say when I instruct you to put a secure watch on the traitor," said Isabella with a damning tone in her voice .

"Yes , M'Lady," said Roquefort Rat in a voice that trembled with as much breakability had it been a porcelain cup and a saucer swiveling on a wood table.

"And how is it?" thought Roquefort Rat, "that one minute he was a simple scribe, a common personality of the rodent genus, who had never been a part of any scheme larger than that of stealing bird eggs from a robbins nest, and now he was suddenly cast into the role of a spy?"

"I will inform you after the rally tonight, 'Rat' whom I wish you to watch," said Isabella with what Roquefort Rat hurtfully concluded was a purposeful splitting of his name in a way to insult him .

After the groupings of soldiers reassembled and the entire Court was at the attention of Princess Isabella, Princess Isabella alliterated a series of her mental notes which outlined her position and purpose for her land holdings, her rule of law, her 'this' and her 'that'.

The "hers" began to mount to such a height of acquisition that a snail from The Marsh of Tuileries whispered to a bullfrog from the same district that if Princess Isabella continued naming any more property her's there would be nothing left that would be left to call 'theirs' .

And then to the great relief of those who were standing at attention Isabella commenced with her speech and sat down allowing Roquefort Rat to tidy up the meeting with miniscule directions and particulars.

Those closest to the throne noticed their princess seemed greatly agitated and watched out of the corner of their eyes as she dug with great energy at the side of her leg.

And that which caused Isabella her agitation was the fact that she had not observed Baron Nelson's presence throughout the entire meeting. Lady Emma of course had the excuse of staying home and lying still so as not to take away her energy from the gestation of children.

But Princess Isabella decided she would suffer no excuse for the tardiness of her Barren save for the very idea that he may have met an enemy cannon ball head on and was suffering with amnesia.

Once the meeting officially concluded the Court began to clear and Princess Isabella looked round for Roquefort Rat whom she noticed had, with unusual haste, put on his coat and hat, gathered his notes and was making his best effort to blend in with the exiting crowd.

"I say , Rat!" shouted Isabella from her throne. And the very nature of her boisterous call, and the idea that she should address one of her subjects in such a vile context, caused the entire shuffling of bodies in the room to halt in their paces with audible gasps emanating from some of their mouths.

"I say," said Princess Isabella as she rose to her feet and began to descend down the stairs in the direction of Roquefort Rat " I do believe we have a meeting scheduled, my dear friend, or have you left your calendar in the gentlemen's room?" (E-gad! The gentlemen's room.)

Had Princess Isabella crossed a barrier that no female British potentate had ever crossed; the making mention of the ' gentleman's room'? Roquefort Rat's right foot began to tap uncontrollably loud as it did every time he became nervous.

Isabella stared piercingly into poor Roquefort Rat's eyes as she stood directly in front of him.

"Well?" she snapped with a sharp demanding tone .

"I assure you Your Highness, my, my, my…" stuttered Roquefort Rat, another uncontrollable response to his feelings of nervousness "my intention was to leave the room for but a few moments while straightened my hair; I did quite want to look pre, pre, presentable for my, my, my Pri, Pri, Princess."

Isabella laughed the poor rodent to scorn. "It would take you more than just a few minutes to straighten all the hairs on your shrewish body. Off with you then I shall employ the help of one of my more adequate subjects," said Isabella watching as Roquefort Rat's body was tottering and in the throes of falling over with the sense that he had been shamed.

Isabella retired to her room that evening dragging her train slowly and purposefully up every wooden step swishing it and wagging it "like a ferocious lizard" she said to herself while smiling like the most elevated of the lizard family: the crocodile.

"And why not a crocodile?" she continued to think as she passed from the third landing onto the fourth flight. "I shall scare them all; Shant' I ?!"

And then with this verbal self assurance there came a pocket of air up out from her belly all the way up her throat and out her mouth that sounded like a dismal roar of a lonesome dog locked in a cage.

"What was that?" questioned Isabella wanting to pretend that the noise she had made had humored her but in reality embarrassed and even terrified her.

By the time Isabella arrived to her room she was successful in convincing herself that the ougr type noise that had come from somewhere deep inside her was nothing more than undigested food commingled with gas.

Isabella dropped her cape and the the rest of her garments one by one onto her bedroom floor knowing her mother would pick them up and went into the bathroom to immerse in the bath water.

She had not removed her tiara as she favored herself with the reminder that she was of royal descent and that she must always be on alert and never not in the 'costume' for her lofty office. The water was particularly warm and soothing and with the extra droplets of bubble bath she had poured in rose around her body like one glass bubble to the effect that Isabella felt as if she must be on a cushion somewhere in the clouds.

She lay her head back on the rim of the tub and imagined for herself that she possessed the ability to control the winds; and these winds she commanded to push her reclining cushion directly over the land of Jolly Old England somewhere in the time earlier in this century and exactly above the residence of David Copperfield .

"Oh what a beautiful sight he is," said Isabella who was very capable of seeing through the walls of his home, "far more handsome than any illustrator had sketched him in any book edition.

And there sitting beside him, coming into to greater focus for Isabella to see, sat a sad, sallow eyed young lady whom Isabella knew could be none other than David's love, Little Emily.

Both David and Emily were weeping as they knew that Emily was soon to leave with her family to Australia and this was their final time of being together . "Would David have embraced me the same as he had not fallen for Little Emily? asked Isabella of herself and then in a wistful, blink of thought, embarked on the image of the young Mr. Copperfield bent at the knee before her as she sat on the couch in the manor, placing an engagement ring upon the fourth finger of her left hand.

"But what am I to say to my mother? asked Isabella of her now betrothed.

"Leave that to me, Dear, said David Copperfield gallantly as he rose to a standing position. "But before I go to see her, my Love, I beg thee to seal our engagement with just one kiss on the lips."

Isabella shut her eyes and arched forward her neck, positioning her head at ever so slight an angle; her lips in a puckering position. But then came the sound of the Pulstar Manor's front door bell which resonated so offensively that the spell of Isabella's dream burst like so many bath bubbles which had lived out their short existence.

Isabella lifted herself from the tub and put a towel around her while simultaneously stepping onto the floor and walked to her bedroom door. There was always a slight creaking sound when she opened her door but the noise would not be detected from the manor entrance hall as there was once again the voice of her mother engaging the presence of a male visitor.

"Yes, Mr. Farnsworth," said Edna, "your Mr. Rancid spoke of you. And yet I am not so sure we,have need of his solicitor going about organizing things from Toad's estate just yet."

But somehow Mr. Farnsworth had maneuvered himself into the drawing room and by the time Isabella put on her clothes and gathered up Dinah the two of them barely caught the end of Mr Farnsworth's silver tongued chicanery while she stood undetected on the other side of the drawing room wall.

"Then I suppose there will not be a problem, Sir," said Edna resignedly," as she offered Mr. Farnsworth a seat. "I will certainly allow you the time you think it will take for you to arbitrate Toad's will and organize everything for as smooth a transfer of the remainder of legal documents." (Oh how I do wish Toad would have included me in his business affairs; I feel so terribly helpless) thought Edna in the same vein as a child who had forgotten to lock the wheels of her wagon and watched as it cascaded down the drive to some degree of wreckage.

Isabella was observing her mother and the visitor Mr. Farnsworth whom we have related previously in our story as a man who cut a rather dashing figure: tall, thin, impeccably dressed with a predisposed demeanor giving him an air of being an authority about any subject he cared to meander on about .

And today Mr. Farnsworth's subject was the subjugation of Edna's mind and the family estate; not that Edna would in any way be aware of Mr. Farnsworth's intentions. Mr. Farnsworth had not survived the many months in Brixton prison and the numerous beatings, the deprivations of all that the base human craves for simple comfort and, not come to a firm understanding of the very fabric of human thinking and knowing how to mold or manipulate it into his own way of reasoning.

This Edna, a society high brow so-and-so, was nothing more to Mr. Farnsworth, prison inmate 0078/cell block 40/second level, than any other genus of a human composition that he would find-out and seduce her central area of weakness.

"Look at her," thought Farnsworth to himself, "gazing off with her eyes to the ceiling like that; a simpleton watching for her departed, winged husband to flutter into view. This subjugation of her loneliness will be nothing more than child's play".

And just at that moment as Farnsworth was reveling in the conquest before him, Dinaha coughed a hair ball up her esophagus to which Anubis responded to by slapping Dinah angrily upon the head.

"Isabella, is that you my dear?" called out Edna in a frail voice as if being in the presence of Mr. Farnsworth had in someway siphoned off much of her energy .

"It is I, Mother," said Anubis. "My friend Isabella has gone to her own home."

There was an unbelievably long, and very tense moment of silence, before all the pieces of the game Isabella was playing came fresh to Edna's mind. "Oh yes, Anubis my dear, please do come in. I wish for you to meet an associate of Mr. Rancid; you remember, the one who befriend our Toad?"

Anubis came round the wall holding Dinah out in front of her as if Dinah were a bit of armor to protect herself from this 'associate'. Farnsworth rose with a great gesture of gentlemanliness and stepped forward with his arm and hand extended "How do you do, young man?" said Farnsworth.

Anubis reached out her hand from the fluff of Dinah's fur intending to engage Farnsworth's hand but with not so much enthusiasm as did Dinah who swiped at Farnsworth slicing open two of his fingers with her claws.

"The Devil!" hissed Farnsworth whose face had crimped in deadly disdain while putting his bloody fingers into his mouth.

"Oh I am so terribly sorry," rang out Mrs. Tumblers as she rose to intercede, while casting an angry look towards Anubis whose head was cocked sideways and showing an attitude on her face expressing complete indifference.

"Wait," said Edna motioning to Farnsworth "and I shall bring a towel."

And as Edna hurried to the hall closet Farnsworth's blasted out to Anubis "Where did you get that damn thing?"

"She came to us as through a looking glass," responded Anubis nonchalantly.

"Ought to throw her in a fountain with a brick tied round her neck," growled Farnsworth as Edna returned with a thick washcloth.

"My dear man, this is hardly the greeting to our home I wish for anyone to receive," groveled Edna. "Come now into the kitchen where we can wash your hand and I can boil you up a serving of tea."

As Edna led the way to the kitchen Farnsworth turned towards Dinaha to give it another hateful glare and was further mortified with Anubis who was still holding one of Dinah's paws and made her kitty wave farewell.

"I am sure he will feel better in the morning, my Sweet," said Anubis to Dinaha while laughing inwardly and wondering if she would be able to inflict any other sufferings on this uninvited associate before the day was through?

On the following morning as the three ladies sat in their respective chairs for breakfast tea , Mrs. Tumblers said to her daughter "Oh, wasn't that a frightful introduction we gave Mr.Farnsworth; I have never seen a person explode with such fury over a few little scratches . He most assuredly does not have a garden of his own or he should be used to having his fingers pricked by thorns and needles. Just the same I have to admit he was quite well versed with his knowledge about deeds and trusts. If only Toad had not been so secretive," said Edna again with a doleful, wistful sigh.

"I don't think Dinah quite liked The Associate mother," said Isabella feeding a small bit of muffin to Dinah and then petting her on the head as she bit upon the morsel.

"That was obvious," said Edna. "And yet I have never have expected her to reach out and claw so viciously; she was obviously abused terribly while in the pound."

"Yes, mother, but you have to remember that Dinah has hardly come in contact with anyone human but yourself and myself; but she does have many friends in the animal kingdom. She gets along marvelously well with Baron Nelson and Lady Emma."

"Whom did you say, my dear?" said Edna looking over the top of her London Times and peering through her glasses.

"Baron Nelson and his wife Lady Emma," said Isabella determinately. She also knows Roquefort Rat; altogether there are probably about one thousand animals and insects she has acquaintance with."

"My child, listen to yourself; here you go on again about something imaginary and allowing it to become a part of your daily existence."

"I must say, Toad and I have not exposed you to the profound tales of classical history; the works of Shakespeare, and Milton, just so you can replace them with stories of whimsical nonsense. And as far as keeping a respectful balance of whom you are speaking, Baron Nelson was one of this country's most decorated naval heroes while this Lady Emma was nothing more than a strumpet!"

Edna went back to reading her Times but apparently Toad's name had been summoned once too often that morning and Edna responded by producing the tissue tucked into the sleeve of her sweater and dabbed it gently at the corner of her eyes and lightly blew her nose.

"No matter how annoying his habits became," whimpered Edna "I shall never forget my beloved Toad."

"Not to worry mother, said Anubis encouragingly (but in reality she said this to keep from laughing as she thought Edna looked very old and immensely pathetic). "Undoubtedly Toad is sitting on a fluffy cloud plucking upon his harp listening and watching all of our activities. And he assuredly is quite touched with our remembrances for him. I will be one to testify that he was altogether a wonderful mate for you. Chin up old girl, you shall be seeing him in less than a fortnight, don't you think?"

After breakfast Edna sat with her legs propped up on her stool while listening to the tense placement of notes from Bach's harpsichord. "Good heavens!" thought Edna while Anubis sat quietly on the carpet bobbing a string up and down for Dinah to jump at.

"I shall be seeing Toad in a fortnight?") Somehow she could not imagine an eternity of Toad and his fussy ways. With him everything had to be 'just so'; from the turning down of the bed at exactly eight every evening and the boiling of his tea water to the precise temperature. She wondered if it were sacrilegious wishing for a life on some other cloud for her? At least there would be the assurance of never having to cook a meal or wash or fold laundry again.

In as little as two weeks Edna had begun to look forward to Mr. Farnsworth' s daily visitations and he showed no little invention with compliments directed at Mrs. Tumbler's self worth. Farnsworth's arrows of deception came directly to the open wound of Edna's mourning heart.

First he was all about the decor of the manor; the coverings of the upholstery and how adequately they complimented the curtains and carpets. And there was quite the celebration when Edna Tumblers presented her family's solicitor with the delicious treats she had prepared for him each night before.

"I am the one least surprised," he said with eloquence of Claudio: the personage he was once fortunate enough to recreate in the staging of

"Much Ado About Nothing", "to find a home so nourished with good taste that it would by naturalistic default lead only to a woman who dressed with such impeccable taste as yourself, Mrs. Tumblers." With which Ms. Tumblers could only respond to his fawning by requesting that Lord Farnsworth from then forward address her as: "Edna".

And once his prey had swooned to defeat; Lord Farnsworth guided by the puppeteer's hand of Mr. Rancid, placed before poor Edna a series of legal documents that given her signature literally stole all that was in her physical possession.

Nothing of Farnsworth's hypnotic performance was lost upon the observations of Anubis. Anubis was completely amused at the seduction of her mother, perhaps not understanding the severity of Lord Farnsworth's skullduggery but saw it as an opportunity to learn for herself the fine art of deceit.

As far as Farnsworth attention towards her, Anubis received an occasional compliment about the sturdiness of his shoulders and how a "fine chap like (himself) could one day find suitable work in a bottle factory sticking on labels with horse glue."

Anubis responded to Farnsworth's condescending remark by saying that his heart's desire was to learn the skills of a detective not unlike Sherlock Holmes and expedite the incarceration of all of London's philanderers and thieves (in so many words).

And so a dynamic of three interacting personalities mingled under the eaves of the Pulstar Manor: Lord Farnsworth's mission was to uncover a most particular item for his enslaver for which item Farnsworth had little knowledge and only vague description.

There was Edna, in her state of shock at the sudden loss of her beloved Toad, whom even at this very writing is falling more and more under the seductive mysteries of One Lord Farnsworth whose tricks of efficatons are more readily available than a stage assistant for the great Svengali.

And then of Anubis, he, one without whom this story would have no flavor; he, a she, once an abandoned child, now the age of twelve, and living the double life of a once dethroned princess who has found her way back to The Court of Forty elected this second time to the equal duties of queen.

But Isabella was not without her awkwardness as she was not only Royalty, but she was also a boy-child named Anubis posing as a nephew under the care of a widowed woman for whom she had no respect.

Both Anubis and Isabella knew only to well that the further their mother drank of the intoxicants of the solicitor Lord Farnsworth the more sure she would find himself/herself an orphan again, perhaps this time left in an elongated raft to float among the bulrushes of the murky Thames.

But then in the midst of turbulent times as humans sometimes find themselves, in open fields engulfed by a wicked tornados, they can simultaneously find themselves in the eye of that turbulence and find it a very calming place. Isabella allowed herself to go up once again to the fourth floor of the Pulstar Manor and to sit upon her bed to meditate and there, after many hours of calm, devised a plan to save Edna against the wiles of the Farnsworth Devil and secure for herself a situation of living where she would never have to face abandonment again.

Anubis first attack upon Farnsworth was to play hide-go-seek with the documents he was building up in Toad's library and confining them to several main files which she left on Toad's desk after Farnsworth left for the evening.

So she reasoned he must take it upon himself to reveal to Edna the truth to, as it were , redirect her mind and emotions and not to be reliant upon Farnsworth simultaneously, exposing his tactics.

Anubis would love to stand just this side of the library doors when Farnsworth entered and soon realized some phantom like entity had shuffled his notes to a point where it may take an hour or more to bring them up to date all the while cursing under his breath but not so loud that Edna would hear. One day Anubis even heard Farnsworth refer to him as "that damn little beast!"

Farnsworth also noticed his teacup which he claims he was given as a gift while in the capitol of Delhi, India as a gift from a Rajah of great renown, had more than once contained at the bottom mixture that looked anything but tea.

Farnsworth once attempted taking a nap on the library sofa only to find upon his awakening his shoe strings tied in knots. "Beast!" he roared again and this time so loud that Edna began to quake nervously until Anubis and her cat came into the kitchen where her mother was sitting.

"It's quite alright Mother," said Anubis to Edna when Farnsworth left for the day. "I have it all under control." This Anubis said while she hand fed his mother, Edna bits of teacake with droppings of honey and cinnamon gotten from the pantry.

"I am beginning to be so afraid of him," said Edna starting to cry. "Every time the doorbell rings I quake with fear."

"He wants us to be afraid of him; don't you see Mother, he is after something he hasn't told us about. He's not just "tidying up loose ends, as he has said. He's no doubt looking for a bit of information written on a piece of paper, something incriminating just like the secret inheritor in Nicholas Nickleby."

"Heavens," whimpered Edna and was about to convulse into a watershed of tears but was interrupted when Anubis took the initiative and pushed more cake in Edna's mouth.

"Should we inform Scotland Yard?" spat out Edna with an odd look of horror in her eyes as crumbs of cake flew forward onto Anubis' body.

"And tell them what, Old Girl; you have given Lord Farnsworth permission to reconnaissance haven't you? What crime shall we accuse him to the Yard for when we don't know ourselves what he's up to?"

Anubis left the plate of unfinished cakes on the table next to Edna as she refused to suffer from the excesses of her mother's futility longer.

"Old Girl," recited Edna to herself after Anubis had left the kitchen. Anubis had also left his Dinah like a hot water bottle on Edna's lap to warm her tummy. "A young girl in my era would have been beaten with a razor strap had she addressed her mother so. But then Isabella tells me she is now once again this Anubis," said Edna wistfully to Dinah. The world has become so topsy-turvy now that my Toad has gone; Oh, what am I to do ... Oh, what am I to do?" she whimpered and then let forth the stimed deluge of tears soaking Dinah's fur.

Several days had past since the shoelace prank and Anubis noticed Farnsworth from that point forward seemed never quite able to relax in his movement or swing with the ease and grace he had originally shown. There were no more attempts at nap taking either and he continued to look around either of his shoulders as if Anubis might sneak up on him with a club.

But in the interim Lord Farnsworth seemed to achieve the intended end in his solicitor roll and never again returned to the Pulstar Manor.

"I believe I have found what it is you were interested in Sir," said Lord Farnsworth as he spoke solicitously to his master Rancid .

Rancid was in no way deceived, nor amused by Farnsworth's faux subservience and simply dismissed him with a wave of the hand and then as if by second thought called out to Farnsworth as he was exiting his study: "Oh, bye-the-bye, you shall be seeing a comparable bonus for all the detective work you have done; and I thank thee greatly!"

Lord Farnsworth bowed grandly at the waist knowing that he had handed his employer a file that was beyond the word "invaluable." Paradoxically though, Farnsworth in no way suspected the nice supplement to his monthly allowance would bring to mind the sage adage of : "you can't take it with you".

Once he was alone Rancid put on his reading glasses and opened the file with as much impatience as a child does when opening his gifts on Christmas morning.

And there it was, marked with copious attention to detail, the inked ledger by the hand

of Dear Old Toad. Had Toad only known what he was collating; the very numbers he thought were hospital supply stock and their transfer and utilization from one department to another were in reality, children; kidnapped children sold as slaves with no more practical end than to

provide Rancid with the lifestyle to which he had accustomed himself to
.

Book IV: As Far as the Mind May Dream

Princess Isabella looked fabulous. She had chosen the full mane of deep
red hair her mother had purchased from an antique dealer who took it in
trade from a woman who desired a piano in the dealer's shop.

Edna did inquire about the history of the wig when she purchased it.

"It was a young lady," the antique dealer reported. "She was born into a
family of limited means and yet they had in their home an inherited
Stefiano piano where her parents gave her music lessons and she had
become quite proficient And then with a series of investments gone bad
her father was forced to sell many of the family valuable home
furnishings to keep from losing the house altogether.

 "The first to go was the piano," explained the woman "and neither I nor
any of my family has been able to afford one after all these many years.")

The piano the young woman inquired about on his show room floor was
in no way the quality of a Stefiano but nonetheless something the woman
emphatically wanted and offered him the amount she said she could pay.
The antique dealer had not been a successful business man for all these
long years and not learned how to be an excellent judge of character .

He knew who was 'working him down' in price even though they could
well afford to pay double what he was asking for on a particular item,
and which persons , such as this most attractive woman with the
strikingly handsome head of long hair, were actually persons with whom
it would be his pleasure to 'come down a bit' on the price.

And so the man talked with the woman, allowed her to sit at the piano,
suggested that she allow herself the freedom of playing a little Chopin
("I don't know if I even remember?") she said embarrassingly as her
fingers lay down on the ivory keys which sunk poetically in response and
began emitting melodic tones her soul had for so many years craved to
hear again…

"What do you think Dinah? said Isabella to her cat who had perched herself like a stool pigeon on a chair next to the full length mirror where Isabella lavished in her own reflection fluffing her fingers through her hair.

"Please, the least you could do is 'meow' once in approval," said Isabella laughing at the dumb beast who was focused on her own appearance and licked her paw and scrubbed her left ear.

And receiving no response from her cat Isabella swung her arm catching Dinah by the head with the back of her hand sending Dinah several feet in the air and onto the floor. "Damn you, you little pile of excrement!" shouted Isabella. "I'll show you how to treat your Queen!"

Dinah lay stunned but uninjured while Isabella fluffed her hair one more time before Isabella grabbed her cape from off the bed, and tied the ribbon firmly around her neck and straightening it upon her shoulders.

"Cat got your tongue?" she said mockingly to Dinah, and then laughed while prancing out of the room.

The Demise of the Court of Forty and the Death of Anubis

"The Court of Forty is now in session," enunciated Pristine Poly a proud parrot whose full flume blazed lavishly under the court chandeliers.

It was none too obvious that Roquefort Rat was not in his usual position acting as scribe and attendant, and there were enough whispers among those present as fears for his whereabouts were enough to fill a Piccadilly street gossip tribunal .

"All rise," continued Pristine Poly whom those standing to his left noticed he snuck a brief glance of vanity at his own reflection in one of the many full length mirrors that had been hung by Isabella's with the purpose of enlarging and enhancing herself and her invented magnificence.

"All rise and let us honor our queen, the Resplendent , the Treasured, The All Wise : Queen Isabella !"

"Good heavens," whispered Tertullian Toad to Farnsworth Finch, "Our Queen seems to have been lifted to yet another plateau in the time of her absence."

"She will reign from such heavenly heights, she will no longer be of any earthly good," said Farnsworth shaking his head in dismal agreement .

Queen Isabella rose from her throne, which had anyone noticed, would have seen that there were numerous jewels mostly of sapphire inserted into the wood armrests and backing of her recently acquired, overly large wood chair painted with an intense gold sheen.

Without so much as a nod of her head to Pristine Parrott, nor even so much as to smile down to those before her, Queen Isabella commenced her brief remarks elongating her neck and thrusting her chin up to the central vault of the roof as if she were challenging the gods themselves .

"We shall endeavor," said Isabella pausing after these first three words, in the very same way she had heard done by the politicians in the House of Commons, " .. . to conquer our enemy; to thrash him until there is nothing left of him, nor his family, nor the memory of any of the above said."

"Where once this surviving son of the King Crab has dared to take arms against my Queendom then he has decided to forsake the very breath that his children's, children should have inherited ."

"Instead they will die before they are conceived . I will rob them of their innocence as they would have rocked in their cradles by the hand of their adorning Nannies, cooed over by their attentive mother's, played with in the ocean waves with their fathers, shown the patterns of the wind currents with those of their same flocks. And from that time forward all the lands whose rulers would think to challenge me, will think rather of the Son of the King Clam and how he came to be crushed and his crustacean self boiled in a post and be made into clam chowder. ! I have spoken."

Queen Isabella sat down , and as she did, Pristine Parrott placed his wings together as a sign that everyone present should follow in applause, hoots, screeches, and stamping of their hooves, or clawing of their feet.

And when the noise in the Court of Forty had settled to a low moan Isabella, who was sitting like a Roman dictator ordering the beheading of a traitorous soldier shouted: "We will march in the morning and those who will not fight with us will certainly die by us!"

It really had been so very taxing for Edna. First there was the death of Toad; then the very presence of Rancid turning up at the front door unannounced was almost too obscene to believe.

There was also this Farnsworth character (if indeed that was his real name?) rummaging through Old Toad's study as if he were a unit of locust chewing to its full the ruin of their manor. And then of course there was Edna's daughter; or was he her "son"? Whoever that person was who occupied the fourth floor turret he, or she, was no doubt possessed by some sort of gypsy demon seed as Toad had said.

At the sheer weight of all these convoluted actions and thoughts , Edna took to fainting spells or so she thought they were. For several days after Farnsworth's final departure Edna would wake up in the middle of the day slouched in any old chair or on the sofa not having remembered lying down at all .

And it came to pass under such strain, Edna began to seek for solace of her troubled soul, which of course meant she did as she always did under times of trouble, she began cooking and eating great gobs of food for distraction.

But after a few days of gorging herself, and hating herself for enduring that bloated feeling, Edna realized that the satiation of her body was not sufficiently realized with food and,made a decision one day that she would go into Toad's study and try another form of sedative. There in his cabinet, behind his desk, were represented a small but very expensive collection of Scotch . Actually, it was smaller than she had remembered; Toad used the liquor rarely, and for the most part only when entertaining an intimate associate . Farnsworth, Edna reasoned, had no doubt taken a few bottles when he was conducting his search, but at least, she said in his favor, he was not so obvious as to empty the entire collection.

Edna poured herself a full glass and took a deep longing look at the liquid before beginning to ingest it. Not since their honeymoon night in the

Glintzmore Hotel had Edna put this substance to her lips. She was always the teetotaler at parties, feeling, she had to admit, a bit superior to all those who imbibed.

Oh those grand days of parties! What an incredibly good time it was to be alive. World War One was over, Toad's career was in full throttle. His father had recently passed, and the Pulstar Manor was all their own.

And Toad; the first time she had seen him was at her best friend's wedding ... not toadie at all!

His profile was striking; chiseled like flint fallen from a mountain side while his full head or black hair glistened as an oil pool under a full moon.

Toad look at her for the very first time; an animal in pursuit; and she, his willing prey caught in the glint of his glare.

After several sips of the Scotch, Edna began feeling a different kind of faltering from the type she had been feeling in Farnsworth's presence. This time it was a euphoria the intensity of which she had not felt since that special, romantic night with the man she had fallen madly in love.

More than handsome Toad was in every way the ultimate romantic. Carrying her across the threshold of their suite while singing sweetly with his lips nestled in her ear. Toad swept his bride into a veritable garden of a room. Sitting on every conceivable surface were the most elaborate floral arrangement each one enhanced with a decorative porcelain vase. And strewn across the bed, hundreds of multicolored rose petals all hand picked by Toad from his own garden.

Candles were burning from brass stands as well, emanating the most luscious aromas. "To us for evermore, my Grecian Goddess!" said Toad as he tipped his glass to his new bride's and winked at her as if he were the Devil himself.

Another drink from the glass and for some reason Edna found herself opening the right top drawer where Toad had kept his cigars and lighter. She felt herself quite bold pulling out the cigar and sniffing at it as she had seen innumerable men do in their jocular ways once they had put themselves to a side room separating themselves from the women they brought with to parties.

But tonight was something of a celebration, and for what she was not sure; Edna took another drink and found she really did not give-a-fig!

Filled with the rush of a multitude of emotions Edna sauntered over to the couch and sat down. Crossing her legs with great style and fluffing at the hem of her skirt and then her hair Edna put down her glass and with he lighter proceeded to light-up the cigar.

"Mother," said Isabella cautiously who had come in softly while Dinah bounded ahead noticing by virtue of her animal instinct that something was patently different in the mood of Edna. "What are you doing, Mother? What is that smell?"

"I do believe Sir Anubis, or whatever it is you are calling yourself these days," said Edna over her shoulder to her daughter, "I am having a bit of a celebration; I'd invite you to share it with me but it is rather a private affair."

"Mother, please," said Isabella walking cautiously to her mother whose body was languid and her cheeks flush gave her daughter a challenging smirk.

"If it's bunny's or kitty' you've come to talk about my dear, you'll find you've come to the wrong drawing room; indeed, you seem to have come to the wrong manner altogether." And with this curt dismissal Edna bounced her head in the direction of the ceiling and let out a flume of smoke.

The disdain Isabella felt for her mother at that moment was a feeling mixed with rage and disgust. Isabella who was being shadowed by Dinah turned from her mother with a nasty invective and simultaneously stepped on poor Dinah's foot . The poor kitty screamed but even with the combination of the two of them, Isabella cursing, and Dinah screeching, Edna was not in the slightest bit amused and took another sip of Scotch and one more puff from her cigar.

Queen Isabella burst into the Court of Forty which sent two large, crow sentinels playing a game with bones and dice in the back of the chamber jumping to their talons and snapping to attention .

"Where in the bloody-hell is everyone?" demanded Isabella, as she pushed furniture out of the way before coming face to beak with the crows.

"They have gone to war, my Queen," said the most stout of the two who cowered into a driveling mass of sticky and frightful sweat .

"Upon whose orders?!" demanded Isabella, this time screaming .

"It was the unanimous decision of the Court lieutenants, my Queen," said the crow who for the first time considered himself fortunate that he had not been elected into one of the more prestigious levels of decision making even though here to for he was constantly complaining about being a simple sentinel .

"Then I will remove their heads, once I catch up to them," said Isabella into the collar of her gown while twisting her lips together as if they were two strands of licorice candy .

Isabella wasted no time in putting changing into her military gear with her flak jacket, side arms and fitting on her helmet . "Make yourselves useful you Crows!" shouted Isabella whom by the putting on of the helmet and went to the boarding dock and climbed into a transport raft with the crows following .

"I am the commander of this craft," said a Turtle Sharp who was considered quite handsome in his own circle of amphibians "be it ever so humble," he said diminutively.

"Spare me the sweet homilies," snapped Isabella "or I'll turn you on your back."

"Yes, M' Lady," said Turtle Sharp whose voice had reduced in volume by as much as half and was lost altogether in the rush of waves.

The journey to the battlefront had seemed less than minutes in the crossing and the sound and the fury of battle wafted across the bow of Isabella's boat long before any of the warrier participants could be seen.

The air was thick with cannon discharge which rolled along the water like a carpet of smog . The crow who was taking the reading from the ship's compass could hardly be trusted with his calculations and Isabella took the chance to stand at the cross deck of the small craft to see if she could observe any movement of the enemy .

Isabella placed one hand on the shell of the tortoise and stood tippity-toes on her wooden seat while coupling her hand at the crest of her brows the way captains of ships do when pictured in paintings or lithographs.

And just then, a round sphere the size of a small comet and traveling just as fast came tumbling down, missing Isabella's boat by mere meters. The missile projectile splashed into the water with such force that even with the sea water undulating to counterbalance the bomb, Isabella fell flat onto her back into the spine of the craft where a pool of water had gathered, soaking her through to the skin.

The crows were quick but, not to quick, to help Isabella to her feet, one winking to the other displaying joy at having seen their nasty potentate lying like a spoonful of applesauce poured and splattered onto the floor . Isabella regained her composure and adjusted her hat once again and, once again stood, this time with both hands on the back of the tortoise shell and he thinking that he could easily bite off several of her fingers were he of a mind to teach Isabella a lesson in humility .

"There!" shouted Isabella releasing one of her hands and pointing off to the starboard side and, then taking the very hand pushing it against Turtle Sharp's head in the direction he was to take the boat .

Fingers, I'm thinking fingers.") thought Turtle Sharp to himself as he maneuvered the ship. Explosions casting forth orange flames could be seen shooting from several of the larger enemy ships which simultaneously bellowed out great curtains of smoke adding to the congestion in the air. There were any number of Isabella's smaller craft with gaping holes bobbing upside down in the water as her boat sped by and directly into the battle. Clinging to many of the wounded craft were fellow sailors calling out to their Queen to save them.

"Expendable ; careless , inexperienced and absolutely ... expendable,") said Isabella within her thoughts regarding her drowning subjects. "Faster," screamed Isabella in Turtle Sharps ears "or I ' ll have the chef make soup of your innards!" ("Fingers, toes, and tongue as well; you surely brat!")

On they pushed at full speed, and directly into the fullness and catastrophe of war. Water churned under the boat as cannon balls fell inches from the frail wooden vessel the water splashing into the little freight with such volume that in the end would be the cause of it sinking.

But then if by destiny, (or if you will, purpose from some unseen Hand) Isabella's boat came directly upon the effigy of the King Crab's ugly crustacean son, whipping and waving in the form of a belligerent, beckoning cloth flag, mocking the very name of Her Majesty, Isabella Rose Tumblers.

The flag waved from the mizzen mast of the crustacean son's private frigate which housed multiple, water line cannons. Each cannon was secured behind its individual door, and when Isabella's boat came within range the doors jumped open .

"Fire!" screamed the ship's gunner commander and a thunderous wall of steel came at Isabella's craft like a steam locomotive engine thrown sideways.

And fire it was; a torturous heat that bleached the skin like acid and with smoke that suffocated, accompanied the confusion and pain with steel portions that snapped bones. Isabella could never have imagined such anguish; how on earthly- hell could any human encounter such sufferings? All Isabella would remember in the days and nights that would follow was her rolling among the rows of Toad's deteriorated garden, writhing in pain and calling out to her mother: "Edna!"

Epilogue

Thomas Dodgson, III was born in London's fashionable Kensington Street not more than a coins toss from the Pulstar Manor. He well knew the privileges of being born into a family of means and yet this did not blind him to the plight of the impoverished.

Indeed Inspector Dodgson of Scotland Yard had seen the ravages of those who had taken up residence on 'the other side'. These would be the communal neighborhoods such as Lancashire known as the infamous Black Country with its landscape of coal and iron fields where Inspector Dodgson had developed a thick skin in response to observing the aftermath of pain inflicted by one 'human' upon another.

And it was he, Inspector Dodgson whom now had as it were a sort of sluth-exclusive reputation for being the one to have traced the footsteps of Rancid for over fifteen year.

He became acquainted with this Rancid gentleman on his first case acting as sergeant second class. It was a case involving the raising of monies to build a school in Devonshire where at the time Rancid was chief council member for that city. The monies were raised but the school was never built. All fingers pointed to Rancid as the one who was the embezzler of the funds and yet he was never put on trial.

"No more an elusive creature is he, " cautioned one of Dodgson's superiors when he had first gone out sleuthing that shadowy figure.

Dodgson found this salient foreboding to true to the extent that he now referred to Rancid as "Creature". His great loathing for Creature came not only for the multiple crimes he was suspected of implementing, but the very idea that he, Inspector Dodgson, was unable to convict Rancid of anyone of them.

As always, no matter how meticulously Dodgson and his staff worked to entangle Creature in his misdeeds, Rancid passed through their traps with nary a wrinkle of shame on his hand-sewn tweeds.

Alas, both men knew whom the other was. In fact they had met several times and it was always Rancid who strode across the ballroom of some fanciful charity event fashioned himself in the latest styled tuxedo and top hat, cane, his hand extended and his charms circulating about him as if he had been sprinkled with the most potent fairy dust needed to cover over his vile deceits.

Dodgson had to admit he was just a little charmed standing in the presence of Creature. Indeed, Creature possessed the uncanny ability of fluffing one's self pride, touching on (and here was the amazing thing!) just that part of yourself which you had self-confidence in least.

He would then massage that weakness with a contrivance of words, pretend it was he alone you could be transparent in front of, and that he thought nothing more of it than had you been a beautiful butterfly gone by with an injured wing.

 ("How was he able to get on ... every crevice of licentiousness Dodgson and his officer's investigated gave them all the more reason to shake their heads in despair as their minds were challenged considered the workings of Creature's huge criminal network?")

"And what of the multiple bodies, Sir?" questioned Captain Ralston, Dodgson's superior as both men sat rigidly in Captain Ralston's office, third floor, Scotland Yard headquarters.

Inspector Dodgson made his reports to his captain mid week at precisely eight A. M.. The first part of the week was jammed with all of the activities that bundled up on the weekend; the pub fights often went to the level of brawlers being bludgeoned to death; thieves found it more convenient to rob residences when families were away visiting relatives and friends, and business conventions that sprawled from Friday through Sunday were siren calls for the most aggressive prostitutes and their handlers

And so Inspector Dodgson faced his superior this Wednesday morning to report about the bodies uncovered at the desecrated Pulstar Manor. "We have the positive identity of Mrs. Tumblers."

"Was she the one responsible for the fire?"

"All evidence of the fire begun points to the library where she lay, Sir; yes. But who was indeed responsible is a matter still under investigation."

"You also report Inspector that she and her 'Toad' had basically dropped out of all of London's

social circle for the last twenty five years; the length of Toad's retirement up and to his death," recounting Inspector Dodgson's report.

 "And you say you did talk with Mr. Tumblers about the murder victim outside their residence approximately two years ago?"

"Yes, Sir. Christmas day to be precise. Mr. Tumblers was quite unnerved about the happenstance and, at the same time very congenial offering to aid us in anyway he could."

"You also indicate that after Mr. Tumblers death Mrs. Tumblers was seen outside the manor only once more the time she visited the animal shelter."

"Yes, she adopted a kitten."

"Naturally; lonely I suppose with the loss of Mr. Tumblers. And the other body; the one lying in the sweetbriar near the West gate? "

"We are still pursuing a positive identity, Sir. We think perhaps, it is Rancid's gentlemen, farnsworth. If it is he, he has aged considerably from his last sighting when he finished his term."

"Oh yes, the elusive Mr. "Lord" Farnsworth, his aging no doubt revealing the signs of his multiple visits to the opium dens. And what was the cause of this his death?"

"A single bullet to the back of the head."

"It looks as though," said Ralston gravely "your Creature- chap has effectively covered his tracks once more."

"Most obviously, Sir. Rancid continues to prove himself a bit too clean for us to hope that the murders will lead to him; we of course will follow up every lead."

"Naturally, Inspector Dodgson." Captain Ralston let a few swipes of the clock drift by before he got to the real item of the morning's meeting with what he assumed would go as just one more chapter in the failed efforts to incarcerate Rancid.

"Look Thomas," said Captain Ralston who rarely addressed any of his officers, and especially none of the senior in rank by their first name, unless he wanted to make the most severe point, "I worry that you feel a personal failure in that you have not been able to catch this Rancid figure. I would put you onto another file but you seem to have worked yourself into being an expert on the man's movements. You should count your victories, Sir. What we have gained is impressive; multiple arrests, several hangings, all due to you and your branch's perseverance."

Dodgson was not moving a muscle and no sounds came from his mouth. His downcast eyes told his superior that despite the level of successes Inspector Dodgson would nary' be satisfied until Rancid was incarcerated.

Captain Ralston stood from his desk and walked around to the front of his desk where he leaned against it with his back side standing directly in front of Dodgson's chair.

"May I offer you a "chin-up-my good-man?" he asked humorously.

Inspector Dodgson's mouth creased a tad. "You haven't added any more information about the girl; all you seem to have is your doctor's estimation that she is somewhere between twelve and fourteen years old with absolutely no indication of her identity . Strange, wouldn't you say? The Tumblers at their age taking in what ... a child off the street?"

"I haven't the foggiest, Sir. She is not of British descent, this is certain." "How so?"

"Bones to large for someone that age and skin of a more, as he puts it: 'tough surface'. She certainly is not of British descent."

"I see," said Captain Ralston touching the tips of his proud, red mustache and twiddling it between his fingers. "And these multiple dolls you found in the sweetbriar; what of it?"

"I crawled in my self Sir; the girl seems to have had something of a little fort for herself. There were a few pieces of doll furniture scattered about and…"

"And what, Inspector?"

Dodgson took in a deep breath letting it out slowly before speaking. "Actually the dolls were not dolls at all."

"Then what?"

"Something more on the order of idols; small objects made with leaves and cloth and cotton held together with twine. They are small figurines that were the semblance of birds or invented animals; I can't be sure. I had Sergeant Dempsey wrap the lot of them. I now have them in my office for deeper contemplation."

"So the girl built for herself a hiding place and made toys to play with; why call them 'idols'...what's to contemplate? Why not simply toys?"

"It was their placement, side by side in semicircular arrangement. All the figures were positioned on what I believe could be nothing other than an alter."

Inspector Dodgson promised to keep his superior up to date on the case the Times chose to call: The Pulstar Murders.

Before going to his next appointment, Dodgson stopped by his favorite pub, receiving greetings from just about everyone. Some of his closest friends patted him on the shoulder knowing the weight he carried with his relentless pursuit of Rancid.

Dodgson took his usual seat at the end of the counter and winked with intrigue at Rita the waitress. The Wednesday cream soup was overly hot again and once again Dodgson burned his tongue.

"When will you ever learn, my Love?" said his devoted wife when he complained about it at late supper that evening.

Lunch was eaten rapidly as if it was an unnecessary evil taking up his time. Inspector Dodgson paid the bill tipping Rita generously and made his way up one block to the trolley. The few miles ride to hospital gave him time to prepare for the unsightly scene he had come to expect of the third floor burn unit.

Doctor Sullivan was busy minding Isabella's bandages and had his back to Inspector Dodgson when he came upon her partially curtained-off bed. In the moments waiting Dodgson looked around at the other beds as the same sense of grief came up upon him the way ghosts might petition him for its lives to be brought back to normal.

"Inspector Dodgson," said Doctor Sullivan having finished with the bandages and taking off his gloves. Both men shook hands nodding their heads in due respect to the others profession as the nurses pulled round the curtain to give Isabella her privacy. Dodgson managed the strength to take one more quick, furtive look at the girl lying in the bed. He had most certainly seen all the grisly remains of gangster's decapitated body parts flung about in alleyways and run down tenements and took measurements from more than one victim whose head was severed off due to a direct gunshot blast to the face. But there was no wretch he had ever seen more horrible than the face of the child peering out to him from under the sheets than the one the press had named: 'The Little Flower Girl' .

Dodgson followed Doctor Sullivan at his invitation for a cup of tea up to his office."You are very good to take such an interest in her recovery," said Doctor Sullivan while handing Dodgson a cup and motioning him with his hand to take a seat.

"The Yard greatly appreciates your accessibility concerning this case."

"Not at all; anything we can do to help, Inspector."

Both men stirred the sugar in their cups; Dodgson having taken two cubes, Doctor Sullivan one, each reflecting upon their exhaustion concerning their professional responsibilities.

"How is your investigation going, Sir?" said Doctor Sullivan being the first one to drink; Dodgson was more careful, his tongue still smarting from the sting of the soup.

"Slow as they all are, Sir. Nothing simple when the Yard is involved; every hair follicle comes up for review in a case like this."

"It has been a pleasure observing you and your men working; England's finest to be sure." "And you and your staff, Sir said Dodgson raising his mug. "And peradventure then again, Sir, might I ask if the girl has volunteered anything?"

"She is still so sedated Inspector; one never knows quite what she is saying when she does attempt to talk; to listen to her is to hear a mixture of The King's English discernibly mixed with a language from another country; perhaps another century, I am really no expert ."

"Quite; none-the-less anything she may allude to a name, a place; anything could be of immeasurable help."

"We are at the ready for that you may be certain; my nurses attend to her twenty four hours a day and have been apprised to write down anything they think she might be saying."

Both men continued drinking relishing their few minutes of respite .

"There is one development though Inspector, one you might find, as we and our staff most certainly do, quite provocative concerning the fire and the effects upon the girl."

"Yes?"

"Strange as it may seem, and if your reports are consistent with the truth, and once again our diagnosis is correct ... " Doctor Sullivan hesitated.

"What?" asked Inspector Dodgson placing his cup on the table next to his chair and arching forward his body enthusiastically .

"As you report the girl was running to the house when the gas line exploded and then the fire scorched her body. The thing is, despite all the damage to her, she can see perfectly now."

"What do you mean "now" Doctor?"

"I have to report that, for the first time in recorded medical history it seems, the girl who was obviously born without sight, now sees."

PART II

The last fragments of sun rays filtered thru Inspector's Dodgson's partially curtained office windows affording an interesting play of dark and light skipping across the Inspector's roll top desk.

The end of an exceedingly laborious day. The last drops of his afternoon tea to be drunk before gathering his papers and cloak to go home. The explanation for the girl and her ability to now see was explained by Doctor Sullivan in that she had been born with cataracts and the intense blaze from the manor burning had literally lifted the sheathing that had covered the child's eyes from birth.

Along the top surface of this large piece of oak furniture the figurines from Isabella's bramblebush hollow were lined in no particular order; each idol shape of unique invention seemed all the more totem in their display now that he had the luxury to observe them singularly and en mass. They were not attractive but it was obvious that great care had been taken in their construction. Obviously not attractive; the girl had only been able to feel her constructions, not see them.

Inspector Dodgson pulled his hands wearily across his face and rubbed at his eyes with the back of each. "What would it be to go through all of your childhood blinded?" he said to himself. "She wouldn't know what she was not seeing."

And just then as the last breath of sun cast its fading beam into the office, it lit upon the figurine at the far end exposing a polished underside showing thru the cloth and twine. Actually the underside had an exceptional brightness.

Inspector jumped from his seat grabbing the figurine idol with his hand ripping the full covering off exposing the most incredible emerald stone.

The End: Book One

In Memory: Princess Emily Rose Bookout

AUTHORS NOTE:

Dear friends: I had no thought of writing about my daughter Emily Rose in the above novel format after she passed away in the year 2007. When I began this story in the ladder months of that year it was originally intended to be a cartoon series of a small orphan girl in New York. (My, how the subconscious mixes the best intentions!)

I thank my Grandmother, Edna, though a native Australian, for her love of British theater who passed this enjoyment of fine acting to her daughter, my mother Patricia Anne, who imparted it to me. I certainly have no desire to translate back to the 1800's with its lack of air conditioning, super food stores, and most especially its less than adequate medicinal cures.

And yet that very time gives me much joy as I muse my imaginary Tom-Tiddler-way through the cobblestone streets of London, observing the (at some levels) quaint culture, and the curious personalities of, Mr. David Copperfield and his first love, Little Emily; Eliza Doolittle and Professor Higgins, as well being quite taken by the mysteries of Holmes and Watson, and the Stevenson story of: Jekyll and Hyde. I should also like to acknowledge Mr. Dodgson the author of Alice, the girl with the furry white kitten and her multiple adventures.

Thank you again for reading this work, one that I have enjoyed writing immensely. Michael Bookout (From my residence: Sacramento, CA 6-9-09)